RETOLD TALES SERIES

P9-CDL-050

RETOLD AMERICAN CLASSICS
VOLUME I

RETOLD AMERICAN CLASSICS
VOLUME 2

RETOLD BRITISH CLASSICS

RETOLD WORLD CLASSICS

RETOLD CLASSIC MYTHS
VOLUME 1

RETOLD CLASSIC MYTHS
VOLUME 2

The Perfection Form Company, Logan, Iowa 51546

CONTRIBUTING WRITERS

Michael A. Benware
B.A. English
English Teacher

Ann Cody
B.A. English
Educational Writer

Robert A. Klimowski
M.A. Reading, B.A. English
English Teacher

Beth Obermiller
M.A. English
Educational Writer

Michele Price
B.A. Communications
Educational Writer

Rebecca Schwartz
M.A. English
English Teacher

Kristen L. Wagner
B.A. English
English Teacher

Mary J. Wagner
M.S. Reading, B.A. English
Reading Coordinator

FIELD TESTERS

Ken Holmes
Lincoln High School
East St. Louis, Illinois

Dawn McDuffie
Mumford High School
Detroit, Michigan

Robert A. Klimowski
Weeks Transitional School
Des Moines, Iowa

Michal Reed
Bartlett Junior High School
Springville, California

RETOLD TALES SERIES

RETOLD BRITISH CLASSICS

THE PERFECTION FORM COMPANY

Editors:
Kathy Myers
Beth Obermiller

Cover Art: Craig Bissell
Book Design: Deb Bell & Dennis Clark
Inside Illustration: Clint Hanson

TABLE
OF CONTENTS

WELCOME TO THE RETOLD BRITISH CLASSICS

Rugby, a Rolls Royce, The Beatles, and fish and chips. What do this game, car, rock group, and food have in common? They're all great British classics.

We call something a classic when it is so well loved that it is saved and passed down to new generations. Classics have been around for a long time, but they're not dusty or out of date. That's because they are brought back to life by each new person who sees and enjoys them.

The *Retold British Classics* are stories written years ago that continue to entertain or influence today. The tales offer exciting plots, important themes, fascinating characters, and powerful language. They are stories that many people have loved to hear and share with one another.

RETOLD UPDATE

This book presents a collection of eight adapted classics. All the colorful, gripping, or comic details of the original stories are here. But longer sentences and paragraphs in the stories have been split up. And some old words have been replaced with modern language.

In addition, a word list has been added at the beginning of each story to make reading easier. Each word defined on that list is printed in dark type within the story. If you forget a word while you're reading, just check the list to review the definition.

You'll also see footnotes at the bottom of some story pages. These notes identify people or places, explain ideas, or even let you in on an author's joke.

Finally, at the end of each tale you'll find a little information about the author. These revealing and sometimes amusing facts will give you insight into a writer's life and work.

When you read the Retold Tales, you bring each story back to life in today's world. We hope you'll discover why the Retold Tales have earned the right to be called British Classics.

THE MONKEY'S PAW

W. W. JACOBS

VOCABULARY PREVIEW

Below is a list of words that appear in the story. Read the list and get to know the words before you start the story.

apathy—disinterest; lack of feeling
compensation—a payment or deed to make up for a loss
confirmation—proof that supports or reinforces a belief
consequences—effects or results
credulity—readiness to believe without solid evidence
expired—died or stopped
frantically—wildly and anxiously
frivolous—silly and playful
groping—searching about by reaching out and feeling
jarred—clashed or conflicted
liability—legal responsibility, especially for wrongdoing
   or losses
maligned—injured by unkind or untrue remarks
mutilated—injured or crippled, especially through the loss
   of an important part
oppressive—difficult to bear; heavy and depressing
poised—balanced or held steady
preoccupied—wrapped up in thoughts and, therefore,
   unaware of other things
presumptuous—overly bold and self-confident
resolution—determination
subdued—toned down and made quieter
talisman—an object thought to have magical powers;
   a charm

THE MONKEY'S PAW

W. W. JACOBS

The Whites have a nice, modest house and a quiet, ordinary life. To them, magic and spirits are simply the stuff of ghost tales.

Or so they think until the monkey's paw falls into their hands. With that ghastly charm, the Whites open the door to supernatural terror.

The night outside was cold and wet. But inside the small parlor of Laburman Villa,[1] the blinds were drawn and the fire burned brightly.

Father and son played a game of chess. The father had ideas that the game demanded daring moves. So he often

---

[1] A villa is a country house, usually large and rich. In this case, the house is comfortable, but not luxurious.

placed his king in dangerous positions on the board. His moves even led the white-haired lady knitting peacefully by the fire to comment.

"Listen to that wind," said Mr. White. He had just seen a fatal mistake he had made. It was too late to take the move back. But, by speaking, he tried to prevent his son, Herbert, from seeing the error.

"I'm listening," said Herbert. He grimly studied the board as he stretched out his hand. "Check."[2]

"I should hardly think that he'd come tonight," said Mr. White. He spoke with his hand **poised** over the board.

"Mate," replied Herbert.

"That's the worst of living so far out," cried Mr. White. His tone was suddenly and unexpectedly violent.

"Of all the beastly, slushy, out-of-the-way places to live, this is the worst. The pathway's a swamp and the road's flooded.

"I don't know what people are thinking about. I suppose because only two houses on the road are rented, they think it doesn't matter."

"Never mind, dear," said Mrs. White soothingly. "Perhaps you'll win the next one."

Mr. White looked up sharply. He was just in time to catch a knowing glance pass between mother and son. The words died away on his lips. He hid a guilty grin in his thin gray beard.

"There he is," said Herbert. The gate banged loudly and heavy footsteps came toward the door.

The old man rose in polite haste. He opened the door and was heard sympathizing with the new arrival. The new arrival also sympathized with himself.

Mrs. White overheard and said, "Tut, tut!" She coughed gently as her husband entered the room. A tall, sturdy man with beady eyes and a red face followed him.

---

[2]The object in chess is to capture the other player's king. "Check" is a warning from one player that the other player's king is in danger. "Mate" (or "checkmate") means the king cannot escape being captured and the game is over.

"Sergeant-Major Morris," Mr. White said, introducing the man.

The sergeant-major shook hands. Then he took a seat by the fire. He watched contentedly while his host got out whiskey and glasses and put a small copper kettle on the fire.

After the third glass, the sergeant-major's eyes got brighter. He began to talk. The little family circle listened eagerly to this visitor from distant lands. He squared his broad shoulders in the chair. Then he spoke of strange scenes and brave deeds. He also told of wars and plagues[3] and strange peoples.

"It's been twenty-one years," said Mr. White. He nodded at his wife and son. "When Morris went away, he was just a young boy in the warehouse. Now look at him."

"He doesn't look as though his travels have harmed him," Mrs. White said politely.

"I'd like to go to India myself," said the old man. "Just to look around a bit, you know."

"It's better where you are," said Morris, shaking his head. He put the empty glass down. Sighing softly, he shook his head again.

"I should like to see those old temples and fakirs[4] and jugglers," said the old man. "What was that you started telling me the other day? Was it about a monkey's paw or something, Morris?"

"Nothing," said Morris hastily. "Anyway, it's nothing worth hearing."

"Monkey's paw?" said Mrs. White curiously.

"Well, it's just a bit of what you might call magic, perhaps," said Morris casually.

His three listeners leaned forward eagerly. The visitor absent-mindedly put his empty glass to his lips. Then he set it down again. His host filled it for him.

Morris fumbled in his pocket. He explained, "To look

[3] A plague is a deadly disease that kills many people in a short time.

[4] Fakirs are Hindu or Muslim beggars. They are religious men and considered to be holy.

at it, it's just an ordinary little paw, dried like a mummy."
He took something out of his pocket and held it out. Mrs.
White drew back with a disgusted look. But her son took
it and examined it curiously.

"And what is there special about it?" asked Mr. White.
He took the paw from his son. After examining it, he placed
it on the table.

"It had a spell put on it by an old fakir," said Morris.
"He was a very holy man. He wanted to show that fate ruled
people's lives. And he wanted to prove that those who interfered with fate did so to their own sorrow.

"So the fakir put a spell on the paw. He gave it the power
to grant three separate men three wishes each."

Their visitor's manner was so impressive that the family
realized that their laughter **jarred** somewhat.

"Well, why don't you make three wishes, sir?" said
Herbert White cleverly.

The soldier stared at him the way that adults usually look
at **presumptuous** youths. "I have," he said quietly. His
blotchy face turned white.

"And did you really have the three wishes granted?"
asked Mrs. White.

"I did," said Morris. His glass tapped against his strong
teeth.

"And has anybody else wished?" asked Mrs. White.

"The first man had his three wishes, yes," was the reply.
"I don't know what the first two were. But the third was
for death. That's how I got the paw."

His tones were so grave that a hush fell upon the group.

"If you've had your three wishes, then it's no good to
you now, Morris," said the old man at last. "What do you
keep it for?"

The soldier shook his head. "A silly impulse, I suppose,"
he said slowly. "I did have some idea of selling it. But I
don't think I will. It has caused enough mischief already.

"Besides, people won't buy it. They think it's a fairy tale, some of them. And those who do think anything of it want to try it first and pay me later."

"What if you could have another three wishes?" said the old man. He eyed Morris closely. "Would you have them?"

"I don't know," said the soldier. "I don't know."

He took the paw and dangled it between his finger and thumb. Then suddenly he threw it onto the fire. White, with a slight cry, bent down and snatched it off.

"Better let it burn," said the soldier solemnly.

"If you don't want it, Morris," said the old man, "give it to me."

"I won't," said his friend stubbornly. "I threw it on the fire. If you keep it, don't blame me for what happens. Toss it on the fire again, like a sensible man."

White shook his head and examined his new possession closely. "How do you do it?" he asked.

"Hold it up in your right hand and wish aloud," said the sergeant-major. "But I warn you of the **consequences**."

"Sounds like the *Arabian Nights*,"[5] said Mrs. White. She rose and began to set the table for supper. "Don't you think you might wish for four pairs of hands for me?" she teased.

Her husband drew the **talisman** from his pocket. Then the family burst into laughter as Morris, with a look of alarm on his face, caught Mr. White by the arm.

"If you must wish," he said gruffly, "wish for something sensible."

Mr. White dropped it back into his pocket. Then, placing chairs, he motioned his friend to the table.

During the business of supper, the talisman was partly forgotten. Afterward, the three sat listening spellbound to more of the soldier's adventures in India.

Much later their guest left to catch the last train. As the door closed behind Morris, Herbert said, "If the tale about

[5]*The Arabian Nights* is an old collection of tales from the Middle East. The stories are filled with magical events.

the paw is as truthful as the others he told us, we won't make much from it."

"Did you give him anything for it, Father?" asked Mrs. White. She watched her husband closely.

"A little something," said Mr. White, blushing slightly. "He didn't want it, but I made him take it. And he urged me again to throw the paw away."

"Of course," said Herbert, with pretended horror. "Why, we're going to be rich and famous and happy. Wish to be an emperor to begin with, Father. Then you won't be henpecked."

Herbert darted round the table chased by his mother. The **maligned** Mrs. White pursued him with a chair slipcover.

Mr. White took the paw from his pocket and eyed it doubtfully. "I don't know what to wish for, and that's a fact," he said slowly. "It seems to me I've got all I want."

Herbert put his arm on his father's shoulder. "If you only could pay off the house. You'd be quite happy then, wouldn't you?" he said. "Well, wish for two hundred pounds then. That'll just do it."

Mr. White held up the talisman. He smiled, embarrassed at his own **credulity**. Herbert sat at the piano and struck a few impressive chords. His solemn face was somewhat spoiled by a wink at his mother.

"I wish for two hundred pounds," said the old man distinctly.

A fine crash from the piano met the words. The chord was interrupted by a trembling cry from the old man. His wife and son ran toward him.

"It moved," he cried. He gazed in disgust at the paw as it lay on the floor. "When I wished, it twisted in my hands like a snake."

"Well, I don't see the money," said Herbert. He picked up the paw and placed it on the table. "And I bet I never will."

"It must have been your imagination, Father," said Mrs. White. She looked at him anxiously.

He shook his head. "Never mind, though. There's no harm done. But it gave me a shock all the same."

They sat down by the fire again while father and son finished their pipes. Outside, the wind was blowing harder than ever. Mr. White jumped nervously when a door banged upstairs.

An unusual and depressing silence settled upon all three. It lasted until the old couple rose to retire for the night.

"I expect you'll find the cash tied up in a bag in the middle of your bed," said Herbert as he said good night. "And there'll be something horrible squatting on top of the closet watching as you pocket your foul gains."

He sat alone in the darkness. Gazing at the dying fire, he saw faces in it. The last face was so horrible and apelike that he gazed at it in amazement.

It got so real that, with a little uneasy laugh, he felt on the table for a glass of water to throw over it. His hand grasped the monkey's paw instead. With a little shiver, he wiped his hand on his coat and went to bed.

Next morning, the winter sun streamed over the breakfast table. In that bright light, Herbert laughed at his fears. The mood of last night was gone. Now there was an air of everyday wholesomeness about the room.

The dirty, shriveled little paw had been carelessly tossed on a cabinet. It lay there as if its virtues were hardly to be believed.

"I suppose all old soldiers are the same," said Mrs. White. "The idea of our listening to such nonsense! How could wishes be granted in this day and age? And if they could, how could two hundred pounds hurt you, Father?"

"Might drop on his head from the sky," said the **frivolous** Herbert.

"Morris said the things happen naturally," said his father. "You might just think it's coincidence."

"Well, don't break into the money before I come back," said Herbert as he rose from the table. "I'm afraid it'll turn you into a mean, greedy man. Then we'd have to kick you out of the family."

His mother laughed. Following Herbert to the door, she watched him walk down the road. Returning to the breakfast table, she thought merrily about her husband's credulity.

All of this did not stop her from scurrying to the door when the postman knocked. Nor did it stop her from muttering about drunken sergeant-majors when she found that the mail was just a tailor's bill.

She brought the topic up again when they sat down to dinner. "I expect Herbert will have some more of his funny remarks when he comes home," she said.

"That's very likely," said Mr. White, pouring himself out some beer. "But even so, the thing moved in my hand. I'll swear to that."

"You thought it did," said the old lady soothingly.

"I say it did," replied the old man. "There was no thought about it. I had just—what's the matter?"

His wife made no reply. She was watching the mysterious movements of a man outside. This stranger was peering in an undecided way at the house. He appeared to be trying to make up his mind to enter.

Mrs. White was still thinking about the two hundred pounds. So naturally she noticed that the stranger was well dressed. She also noted his silk hat was shiny and new.

Three times the man paused at the gate. Then he began to walk on by.

The fourth time he stood with his hand upon the gate. Then, with sudden **resolution**, he flung the gate open and walked up the path.

At the same moment, Mrs. White placed her hands behind her. She hurriedly untied her apron and put it beneath a chair cushion.

She brought the stranger into the room. He seemed ill at ease. He gazed at Mrs. White out of the corner of his eye. And he listened in a **preoccupied** way as she apologized for the room's appearance and her husband's coat. She explained that he usually only wore it in the garden.

Mrs. White then waited patiently for the stranger to bring up his business. But he was, at first, strangely silent.

"I—was asked to call," he said at last. He stooped down and picked a piece of cotton from his trousers. "I come from Maw and Meggins."

The old lady jumped. "Is anything the matter?" she asked breathlessly. "Has anything happened to Herbert? What is it? What is it?"

Her husband stepped in. "There, there, Mother," he said hastily. "Sit down, and don't jump to conclusions. You've not brought bad news, I'm sure, sir." He eyed the stranger hopefully.

"I'm sorry—" began the visitor.

"Is he hurt?" demanded the mother.

The visitor bowed in agreement. "Badly hurt," he said quietly. "But he is not in any pain."

"Oh, thank God!" said the old woman, clasping her hands. "Thank God for that! Thank—"

She stopped suddenly as the sinister meaning of the man's words dawned upon her. She saw the awful **confirmation** of her fears when the man turned his face away.

Catching her breath, she turned to her slower-witted husband. She laid her trembling old hand upon his. There was a long silence.

"He was caught in the machinery," said the visitor at last, in a low voice.

"Caught in the machinery," repeated Mr. White in a dazed manner. "Yes."

He sat staring blankly out the window. He took his wife's hand between his own. He pressed it as he used to do when they were courting nearly forty years ago.

"He was the only one left to us," he said, turning gently to the visitor. "It is hard."

The other coughed. Rising, he walked slowly to the window. "The firm wished me to express their sincere sympathy with you in your great loss," he said. He spoke without looking round.

"I beg that you will understand I am only their employee. I am merely obeying orders."

There was no reply. The old woman's face was white, her eyes staring. Her breath could not be heard. On the husband's face was a look such as the sergeant might have carried into his first battle.

"I am to say that Maw and Meggins refuse to take any responsibility," continued the stranger. "They admit no **liability** at all.

"But, out of regard for your son's services, they want to make a gesture. They wish to present you with a certain sum as **compensation**."

Mr. White dropped his wife's hand. Rising to his feet, he gazed in horror at his visitor. His dry lips shaped the words, "How much?"

"Two hundred pounds," was the answer.

Unconscious of his wife's shriek, the old man smiled faintly. He reached out his hands and dropped in a heap on the floor.

The huge new cemetery lay some two miles away. There the Whites buried their dead son. Then they came back to a house full of shadow and silence.

It was all over so quickly that at first they could hardly realize it. They continued to wait, as though expecting something else to happen. They waited for something which would lighten this load, too heavy for old hearts to bear.

But the days passed. Expectation turned into acceptance. It was the hopeless acceptance of the old, sometimes mistaken for **apathy**.

Sometimes they hardly exchanged a word. Now they had nothing to talk about. Their days were wearingly long.

About a week after that, the old man woke suddenly in the night. He stretched out his hand and found himself alone.

The room was in darkness. The sound of **subdued** weeping came from the window. Raising himself in bed, he listened.

"Come back," he said tenderly. "You will be cold."

"It is colder for my son," said the old woman. She wept again.

The sound of her sobs died away on his ears. The bed was warm and his eyes heavy with sleep. He dozed restlessly and then slept. A sudden wild cry from his wife awoke him with a start.

"The monkey's paw!" she cried wildly. "The monkey's paw!"

He started up in alarm. "Where? Where is it? What's the matter?"

She came stumbling across the room toward him. "I want it," she said quietly. "You haven't destroyed it, have you?"

"It's in the parlor, on the shelf over the fireplace," he replied, wondering. "Why?"

She cried and laughed at the same time. Bending over, she kissed his cheek.

"I only just thought of it," she said hysterically. "Why didn't I think of it before? Why didn't you think of it?"

"Think of what?" he questioned.

"The other two wishes," she replied rapidly. "We've only had one."

"Was that not enough?" he demanded fiercely.

"No," she cried in triumph. "We'll have one more. Go down and get it quickly. Wish our boy alive again."

The man sat up in bed. He flung the covers from his shaking limbs. "Good God, you are mad!" he cried, horrified.

"Get it," she panted. "Get it quickly. And wish! Oh, my boy, my boy!"

Her husband struck a match and lit the candle. "Get back to bed," he said trembling. "You don't know what you are saying."

"We had the first wish granted," said the old woman in a feverish voice. "Why not the second?"

"A coincidence," stammered the old man.

"Go and get it and wish," cried the old woman. She dragged him toward the door.

He went down in the darkness and felt his way to the parlor. Then he found the mantlepiece. The talisman was in its place.

He was seized by a horrible fear. What if the unspoken wish brought back his **mutilated** son before he could escape from the room?

He caught his breath as he realized he had lost the direction of the door. His brow was cold with sweat as he felt his way round the table. He finally found himself in the small hallway with the unwholesome thing in his hand.

Even his wife's face seemed changed as he entered the room. It was white and expectant. To his fearful mind, she seemed to have an unnatural look upon her face. He was afraid of her.

"Wish!" she cried, in a strong voice.

"It is foolish and wicked," he hesitated.

"Wish!" repeated his wife.

He raised his hand. "I wish my son alive again."

The talisman fell to the floor, and he looked at it with horror. Then he sank trembling into a chair. But the old woman, with burning eyes, walked to the window and raised the blind.

He sat until he was chilled with cold. Now and again, he glanced at the figure of the woman peering through the window.

The candle had burnt below the rim of the china candlestick. It threw fluttering shadows on the ceiling and walls. Finally, with a flicker larger than the rest, it **expired**.

The old man sighed with unspeakable relief at the failure of the talisman. And he crept back to his bed.

A minute or two passed. Then the old woman came silently and apathetically to bed beside him.

Neither spoke. But both lay silently listening to the ticking of the clock. A stair creaked. A squeaky mouse scurried noisily through the wall.

The darkness was **oppressive**. The husband finally screwed up his courage and took the box of matches. Striking one, he went downstairs for a candle.

At the foot of the stairs the match went out. He paused to strike another. At that moment, a knock—so quiet and stealthy it was hardly heard—sounded on the front door.

The matches fell from his hand. He stood motionless, holding his breath until the knock was repeated. Then he turned and fled back to his room, closing the door behind him.

A third knock sounded throughout the house.

"*What's that?*" cried the old woman, startled.

"A rat," said the old man in a shaking voice. "A rat. It passed me on the stairs."

His wife sat up in bed listening. A loud knock echoed through the house.

"It's Herbert!" she screamed. "It's Herbert!"

She ran to the door. But her husband was quicker.

Catching her by the arm, he held her tightly.

"What are you going to do?" he whispered hoarsely.

"It's my boy. It's Herbert!" she cried, struggling. "I forgot it was two miles away. What are you holding me for? Let go. I must open the door."

"For God's sake, don't let it in," cried the old man, trembling.

"You're afraid of your own son," she cried, still struggling. "Let me go. I'm coming, Herbert. I'm coming."

There was another knock and another. The old woman with a sudden jerk broke free and ran from the room.

Her husband followed to the landing. He called after her in a pleading voice as she hurried downstairs.

He heard the chain rattle back. The sound of the bottom bolt as it was pulled from its socket followed. Then came the sound of the old woman's voice, strained and panting.

"The bolt," she cried loudly. "Come down. I can't reach it."

But her husband was on his hands and knees on the floor, **groping** wildly for the paw. If he could only find it before the thing outside got in.

A thunderstorm of knocks echoed through the house. He heard the scraping of a chair as his wife put it against the door. He heard the creaking of a bolt as it came slowly back.

At the same moment, he found the monkey's paw. **Frantically** he breathed his third and last wish.

The knocking ceased suddenly, although its echoes were still in the house. He heard the chair drawn back and the door opened. A cold wind rushed up the staircase.

A long, loud wail of disappointment and misery from his wife gave him courage to run down to her side. From there he darted to the gate beyond. The flickering street lamp shone on a quiet and deserted road.

"The Monkey's Paw" was first published in 1902.

INSIGHTS INTO
W. W. JACOBS

(1863-1943)

William Wymark Jacobs hated crowds. In fact, he preferred the company of only one or two close friends.

In a crowd, Jacobs seemed shy and somewhat sad. But with friends, Jacobs—or "W. W." as he was called—was known as a witty, humorous man.

Critics have often compared Jacobs to another master of the short story: O. Henry. Jacobs' most famous works are horror stories and humorous tales about sailors in port and night watchmen on dock patrol.

These tales were enjoyed by the public. Reviewers generally praised them too. However, once a critic said that the Night Watchman in Jacobs' stories had grown too chatty and easygoing. Jacobs retorted that the critic was way off the mark.

Jacobs' son-in-law, Alec, backed up the writer. He said that the Night Watchman's dialogue was, as always, biting and to the point. He also said the source for Jacobs' sarcastic dialogue was Jacobs' own quarrels with his wife.

Jacobs grew up in London in an area next to the Thames River. As a child, he enjoyed running free beside the river with his brothers and sisters.

Jacobs had plenty of company on those romps. He came from a large family. The Jacobs were also poor. Despite this, Jacobs managed to be admitted to a private school and then college.

continued

Jacobs feared poverty. So he worked hard in school to get a government job. Then when he was sixteen, he began work as a clerk in a savings and loan bank.

This job did nothing to fulfill Jacobs' dream of being a full-time writer. But his dread of poverty made him stick with the job. In his spare time, Jacobs wrote.

By 1899 Jacobs had published three books and many short stories. His name was well known, he had a loyal audience, and critics praised him. At last he felt he could earn a decent living as a writer. So, twenty years after he began, Jacobs finally quit his bank job and saw his dream come true.

As a popular author, Jacobs could ask for high prices from his publishers. He once boasted that he was more highly paid than any other writer except one: Rudyard Kipling.

Jacobs knew how to drive a hard bargain for his work. Even with his first collection of stories, *Many Cargoes,* he refused the publisher's standard price. Instead, he demanded royalties as well as a lump sum.

This kind of arrangement was only made with the famous writers of the day. Jacobs was still a minor author at the time. However, Jacobs could and did make such demands because he produced entertaining, quality tales.

Other works by Jacobs:
"A Change of Treatment," short story
"The Skipper's Wooing," short story
Beauty and the Barge, play
Sunwich Port, novel

THE RED-HEADED LEAGUE
ARTHUR CONAN DOYLE

VOCABULARY PREVIEW

Below is a list of words that appear in the story. Read the list and get to know the words before you start the story.

absorbing—interesting and involving
astuteness—sharp wit and judgment
benefactor—one who aids by giving money or other help
candid—frank and open
deference—polite respect for the views or desires of others
dejected—discouraged and depressed
dissolved—broken up or ended
eligible—qualified to be chosen; acceptable
forfeit—to give up or pay something as a penalty
introspective—concerning the examination of one's thoughts
judicial—able to give a judgment (usually a wise one)
misgivings—fears or doubts
pompous—trying to seem important; stuffy
rogue—rascal or villain
serenely—calmly and quietly
stagnant—showing no activity or motion
tenacious—sticking or holding firmly to something; stubborn
terminated—ended
vacancy—empty or unoccupied place
vulnerable—able to be attacked, injured, or otherwise put in danger

THE RED-HEADED LEAGUE

A poor pawnbroker receives an unexpected job offer—and just because his hair is red.

However, detective Sherlock Holmes sees more in the pawnbroker's case than an amusing tale. He suspects that at the bottom of the deal is one of the most daring criminals in London. Holmes must "dig up" this mastermind before the crime of the century is committed.

I had called upon my friend, Mr. Sherlock Holmes, one day in the autumn of last year. I found him talking intently with another man. The visitor was a stout, red-faced old gentleman with fiery red hair.

ARTHUR CONAN DOYLE

I apologized for interrupting and was about to leave. But Holmes pulled me abruptly into the room and closed the door behind me.

"You could not possibly have come at a better time, my dear Watson," he said, warmly.

"I was afraid that you were busy."

"So I am. Very much so."

"Then I can wait in the next room."

"Not at all, Watson," Holmes said. "Mr. Wilson, I'd like you to meet Dr. Watson. Watson has been my partner and helper in many of my most successful cases. I have no doubt that he also will be of the greatest use to me in yours."

The stout gentleman half rose from his chair and gave a bob of greeting. I noted a quick little questioning glance in his small eyes circled in fat.

"Try the couch," said Holmes, sitting back down into his armchair. He put his fingertips together, as was his custom when in **judicial** moods.

"I know, my dear Watson, that you share my love of all that is bizarre and outside the common, humdrum routine of everyday life. Your enthusiasm has led you to record, and—if you will excuse my saying so—somewhat exaggerate many of my little adventures."

"Your cases have indeed been of great interest to me," I observed.

"Remember my remark from the other day? Just before we set about solving the simple problem of Miss Mary Sutherland's case? I said that for strange effects and odd mixes we must go to life itself. It is always far more daring than any effort of the imagination."

"A statement which I took the liberty of doubting."

"You did, doctor. But none the less, you must come round to my view. Otherwise I shall keep piling fact upon fact on you until your reason breaks down. Then you will say I am right.

"Now, Mr. Jabez Wilson here has been good enough to call upon me this morning. He has begun a story which promises to be one of the oddest which I have listened to for some time.

"You have heard me remark that the strangest things are often connected with the smaller, not the larger crimes. Sometimes, indeed, there is room to doubt whether any real crime has been committed.

"From what I have heard so far, I cannot say if the present case is an example of crime or not. But the events are certainly among the most bizarre that I have ever listened to.

"Perhaps, Mr. Wilson, you would have the great kindness to begin your story again. I ask you not merely because my friend, Dr. Watson, missed the opening part. You see, the peculiar nature of the story makes me anxious to have every possible detail from your lips.

"As a rule, when I have heard a few details, I am able to guide myself by the thousands of other similar cases which I can recall. In the present case I am forced to admit that the facts are, to the best of my belief, unique."

The plump client puffed out his chest with pride. Then he pulled a dirty and wrinkled newspaper from the inside pocket of his overcoat.

He glanced down the ad column, with his head thrust forward and the paper flattened out upon his knee. While he was reading, I took a good look at him. I tried to search for clues in his dress or appearance, as Holmes would do.

However, I did not gain very much by my inspection. Our visitor bore every mark of being an average, commonplace British tradesman. He was fat, **pompous**, and slow. He wore rather baggy gray check trousers and a not overly clean black coat, unbuttoned in the front.

Over his shirt he wore a drab vest with a heavy brass chain. A square, pierced bit of metal dangled down as an ornament from the vest chain. An old top hat and a faded brown overcoat with a wrinkled velvet collar lay upon a chair beside him.

All in all, no matter how I examined him, there was nothing remarkable about the man. Only his blazing red head and the expression of extreme annoyance and discontent upon his face made him stand out.

Sherlock Holmes' quick eye saw what I was doing. He shook his head with a smile as he noticed my questioning glances.

"Beyond the obvious facts that he was once a laborer, takes snuff, is a Freemason,[1] has been in China, and has done much writing lately, I can conclude nothing," said Holmes.

Mr. Jabez Wilson jumped up from his chair. His forefinger was on the paper, but his eyes were upon my companion.

"How in the name of good fortune did you know all that, Mr. Holmes?" he asked. "How did you know, for example, that I was once a laborer? It's the gospel truth, for I began as a ship's carpenter."

"Your hands, my dear sir. Your right hand is a size larger than your left. You have worked with it and the muscles are more developed."

"Well, the snuff then and the Freemasonry?"

"I won't insult your intelligence by telling you how I read that. Especially as, rather against the strict rules of your order, you use an arc and compass breastpin."

"Ah, of course, I forgot that. But the writing?"

"What else can that right cuff mean? It is very shiny for five inches. And on the left sleeve can be seen a smooth patch near the elbow where you rest it upon the desk."

"Well, but China?"

"The fish which you have tattooed just above your wrist could only have been done in China. I have made a small study of tattoo marks and even added to the literature on

[1]Freemasons are members of a secret society. The group promotes brotherhood, morality, and charity. It began as an association of builders. The arc and compass—tools of the architect—still serve as symbols of the group.

the subject. That trick of staining the fishes' scales a delicate pink is unique to China. When I also see a Chinese coin hanging from your watch chain, the matter becomes even more simple.''

Mr. Jabez Wilson laughed heartily. ''Well, I never!'' said he. ''I thought at first that you had done something clever. But I see that there was nothing in it after all.''

''I begin to think, Watson,'' said Holmes, ''that I make a mistake in explaining. *Omne ignotum pro magnifico,* you know.[2] My poor little reputation, such as it is, will be shipwrecked if I am so **candid**. Can you not find the advertisement, Mr. Wilson?''

''Yes, I have got it now,'' he answered with his thick, red finger planted halfway down the column. ''Here it is. This is what began it all. You just read it for yourself, sir.''

I took the paper from him and read as follows.

> TO THE RED-HEADED LEAGUE: On account of the bequest[3] of the late Ezekiah Hopkins of Lebanon, Pa., USA, there is now another **vacancy** open. This job pays a member of the League a salary of four pounds[4] a week for a very small amount of work.
>
> All red-headed men who are sound in body and mind and over twenty-one are **eligible**. Apply in person on Monday at eleven o'clock to Duncan Ross at the offices of the League, 7 Pope's Court, Fleet Street.

''What on earth does this mean?'' I cried after I had twice read the extraordinary announcement.

Holmes chuckled and wiggled in his chair as was his habit when in high spirits. ''It is a little off the beaten track, isn't it?'' said he.

''And now, Mr. Wilson, off you go at the start. Tell us all about yourself, your household, and the effect which this

---

[2]The phrase is Latin for ''whatever is unknown is marvelous.''

[3]A bequest is money or property left by a person in a will.

[4]A pound is an English unit of money.

ad had upon your fortunes. You will first make a note, doctor, of the paper and the date."

"It is *The Morning Chronicle* of April 27, 1890. Just two months ago."

"Very good. Now, Mr. Wilson."

"Well, it is just as I have been telling you, Mr. Sherlock Holmes," said Jabez Wilson, mopping his forehead. "I have a small pawnbroker's business at Coburg Square, near the City.[5] It's not a very large place. Lately, it has not done more than just give me a living.

"I used to be able to keep two assistants. Now I only keep one. And I would have trouble paying him if he wasn't willing to work for half wages, so as to learn the business."

"What is the name of this obliging youth?" asked Sherlock Holmes.

"His name is Vincent Spaulding, and he's not such a youth either. It's hard to say his age. I could not wish for a smarter assistant, Mr. Holmes. And I know very well that he could do better for himself and earn twice what I can give him. But, after all, if he is satisfied, why should I put ideas in his head?"

"Why, indeed? You seem most fortunate in having an employee who comes under the full market price. It is not a common experience among employers these days. Your assistant may be as remarkable as your ad."

"Oh, he has his faults, too," said Mr. Wilson. "Never was such a fellow for photography. Snapping away with a camera when he ought to be improving his mind. Then he's always diving down into the cellar like a rabbit into its hole to develop his pictures.

"That is his main fault. But, on the whole, he's a good worker. There's no vice in him."

"He is still with you, I assume?"

"Yes, sir. He and a girl of fourteen, who does a bit of simple cooking and keeps the place clean. That's all I have

---

[5]The City of London is the name of one district in Greater London (usually just called London).

in the house, for I am a widower and never had any family.

"We live very quietly, sir, the three of us. We keep a roof over our heads and pay our debts, if we do nothing more.

"The first thing that changed that was this ad. Spaulding, he came down into the office just this day eight weeks ago. He had this very paper in his hand.

"He says, 'I wish to the Lord, Mr. Wilson, that I was a red-headed man.'

" 'Why that?' I asks.

" 'Why,' says he, 'here's another vacancy in the League of the Red-headed Men. It's worth quite a small fortune to any man who gets it. I understand there are more vacancies than there are men. The trustees[6] are at their wits' end what to do with the money. If my hair would only change color, here'd be a cozy little place all ready for me to step into.'

" 'Why, what is it, then?' I asked. You see, Mr. Holmes, I am a very stay-at-home man. Since my business came to me instead of my having to go to it, I often went for weeks without putting my foot over the door mat. So I didn't know much of what was going on outside. And I was always glad of a bit of news.

" 'Have you never heard of the League of the Red-headed Men?' he asked with his eyes wide.

" 'Never.'

" 'Why, I wonder at that. You are eligible yourself—for one of the vacancies.'

" 'And what are they worth?' I asked.

" 'Oh, merely a couple of hundred a year. But the work is easy, and it need not interfere very much with one's other occupations.'

"Well, you can easily see how that made me prick up my ears. The business has not been very good for some years. An extra couple of hundred would have been very handy.

" 'Tell me all about it,' said I.

---

[6]Trustees are people who manage property or business for another.

" 'Well,' said he, showing me the ad, 'you can see for yourself that the League has a vacancy. There is the address where you should apply for information.

" 'As far as I can make out, the League was founded by an American millionaire, Ezekiah Hopkins. He was very odd in his ways. He was himself red-headed, and he had a great sympathy for all red-headed men.

" 'So when he died, he left his enormous fortune in the hands of trustees. He instructed them to apply the interest toward providing easy jobs to red-headed men. From all I hear, it pays splendidly and there's very little to do.'

" 'But,' said I, 'there would be millions of red-headed men who would apply.'

" 'Not so many as you might think,' he answered. 'You see, only Londoners who are grown men can apply. This American had started from London when he was young. He wanted to do the old town a good turn.

" 'Then, again, I have heard it is no use your applying if your hair is light red or dark red. It must be real, bright, blazing, fiery red.

" 'Now, if you cared to apply, Mr. Wilson, you could just walk in. But perhaps it would hardly be worth your while to put yourself out of the way for the sake of a few hundred pounds.'

"Now it is a fact, gentlemen, as you may see for yourselves, that my hair is a very full and rich tint. So it seemed to me that, if there was to be any competition in the matter, I stood as good a chance as any man that I had ever met.

"Vincent Spaulding seemed to know so much about it that I thought he might prove useful. So I told him to close up shop for the day and come with me.

"He was very willing to have a holiday. So we shut the business up and started off for the address that was given in the ad.

"I never hope to see such a sight as that again, Mr. Holmes. From north, south, east, and west, every man who had a shade of red in his hair had tramped into the City to answer the ad.

"Fleet Street was choked with red-headed folk. Pope's Court looked like a fruitseller's orange cart. I should not have thought there were so many in the whole country as answered that single ad.

"Every shade of color they were—straw, lemon, orange, brick, Irish setter, liver, clay. But, as Spaulding said, there were not many who had the real, sharp, flame-colored tint.

"When I saw how many were waiting, I would have given up in despair. But Spaulding would not hear of it. How he did it, I could not imagine. But he pushed and pulled and butted until he got me through the crowd. We went right to the steps which led to the office.

There was a double stream upon the stair. Some were going up in hope and some coming back **dejected**. But we crowded in as well as we could and soon found ourselves in the office."

"Your experience has been a most entertaining one," remarked Holmes as his client paused and refreshed his memory with a huge pinch of snuff. "Please continue your very interesting statement."

"There was nothing in the office but a couple of wooden chairs and a table. Behind that sat a small man with a head that was even redder than mine. He said a few words to each candidate who came up. Then he always managed to find some fault in them which would rule them out. Getting a vacancy did not seem to be such a very easy matter after all.

"However, when our turn came, the little man was much more favorable to me than to any of the others. He closed the door as we entered, so that he might have a private word with us.

" 'This is Mr. Jabez Wilson,' said my assistant. 'He is

willing to fill an opening in the League.'

" 'And he is admirably suited for it,' the other answered. 'He has every requirement. I cannot recall when I have seen anything so fine.'

"He took a step backward and cocked his head on one side. He gazed at my hair until I felt quite bashful. Then suddenly he plunged forward, shook my hand, and congratulated me warmly on my success.

" 'It would be injustice to hesitate,' said he. 'However, I am sure you will excuse me for taking an obvious precaution.'

"With that he seized my hair in both his hands. He tugged until I yelled with the pain.

" 'There are tears in your eyes,' said he as he released me. 'I perceive that everything is as it should be. But we have to be careful. We have twice been deceived by wigs and once by paint. I could tell you tales of shoemaker's polish which would make you disgusted with human nature.'

"He stepped over to the window and shouted through it at the top of his voice that the vacancy was filled. A groan of disappointment came up from below. The folk all trooped away in different directions. Finally there was not a red head to be seen except my own and the manager's.

" 'My name,' said he, 'is Mr. Duncan Ross. I am myself one of those hired because of the fund left by our noble **benefactor**. Are you a married man, Mr. Wilson? Have you a family?'

"I answered that I had not.

"His face fell immediately.

" 'Dear me!' he said, gravely, 'that is very serious indeed! I am sorry to hear you say that. The fund was, of course, for the breeding and spread of redheads as well as for their support. It is very unfortunate that you are a bachelor.'

"My face lengthened at this, Mr. Holmes. I thought that I was not to have the vacancy after all. But, after thinking it over for a few minutes, he said that it would be all right.

" 'In another case,' said he, 'the objection might rule you out. But we must stretch a point in favor of a man with such a head of hair as yours. When shall you be able to start your new duties?'

" 'Well, it is a little awkward. I have a business already,' said I.

" 'Oh, never mind about that, Mr. Wilson!' said Vincent Spaulding. 'I shall be able to look after that for you.'

" 'What would be the hours?' I asked.

" 'Ten to two.'

"Now a pawnbroker's business is mostly done in the evening, Mr. Holmes. Thursday and Friday evenings—which are just before payday—are the heaviest. So it suited me very well. My assistant was a good man, and he would see to anything that turned up.

" 'That would suit me very well,' said I. 'And the pay?'

" 'Is four pounds a week.'

" 'And the work?'

" 'Is just a formality.'

" 'What do you call just a formality?'

" 'Well, you have to be in the office—or at least in the building—the whole time. If you leave, you must **forfeit** your whole position forever. The will is very clear upon that point. You don't meet the conditions if you budge from the office during that time.'

" 'It's only four hours a day, and I should not think of leaving,' said I.

" 'No excuse will be accepted,' said Mr. Duncan Ross. 'Neither sickness nor business nor anything else. There you must stay, or you lose your place.'

" 'And the work?'

" 'Is to copy out the *Encyclopaedia Britannica*. There is the first volume of it. You must find your own ink, pens, and paper, but we provide this table and chair. Will you be ready tomorrow?'

" 'Certainly,' I answered.

" 'Then goodbye, Mr. Jabez Wilson. And let me congratulate you once more on the important position which you have been fortunate enough to gain.'

"He bowed to me as I left the room. I went home with my assistant. I hardly knew what to say or do, I was so pleased at my own good fortune.

"Well, I thought over the matter all day. By evening I was in low spirits again. I had persuaded myself that the whole affair must be some great hoax or fraud, though what its object might be I could not imagine.

"It seemed beyond belief that anyone could make such a will. And it seemed incredible that they would pay such a sum for doing anything so simple as copying the *Encyclopaedia Britannica*.

"Vincent Spaulding did what he could to cheer me up. But by bedtime I had reasoned myself out of the whole thing.

"However, in the morning I determined to have a look at it anyhow. So I bought a penny bottle of ink. With a pen and seven sheets of paper, I started off for Pope's Court.

"Well, to my surprise and delight everything was as right as possible. The table was set out ready for me. Mr. Duncan Ross was there to see that I got off to work. He started me off upon the letter A, and then he left me. But he said he would drop in from time to time to see that everything was all right.

"At two o'clock he returned. He complimented me upon the amount that I had written. Then he locked the door of the office after me.

"This went on day after day, Mr. Holmes. On Saturday the manager came in and planked down four golden coins for my week's work.

"It was the same next week and the week after. Every morning I was there at ten. Every afternoon I left at two.

"By degrees Mr. Duncan Ross took to coming in only

once a morning. Then, after a time, he did not come in at all.

"Still, of course, I never dared to leave the room for an instant. I was not sure when he might come. And the place was such a good one and suited me so well that I would not risk losing it.

"Eight weeks passed away like this. I had written about Abbots, Archery, Armor, Architecture, and Attica. With hard work, I hoped that I might get on to the B's before very long.

"It cost me a pretty penny in paper, and I had nearly filled a shelf with my writings. Then suddenly the whole business came to an end."

"To an end?"

"Yes, sir. And no later than this morning. I went to my work as usual at ten o'clock. But the door was shut and locked. A little square of cardboard had been hammered onto the middle of the panel with a tack. Here it is. You can read for yourself."

He held up a piece of white cardboard, about the size of a sheet of notepaper. It read in the following way.

THE RED-HEADED LEAGUE IS
DISSOLVED.
Oct. 9, 1890.

Sherlock Holmes and I surveyed this brief announcement and the sheepish face behind it. Finally the comical side of the affair so completely overcame us that we both burst out into a roar of laughter.

"I cannot see that there is anything very funny," cried our client. He flushed up to the roots of his flaming hair. "If you can do nothing better than laugh at me, I can go elsewhere."

"No, no," cried Holmes. He quickly shoved him back into the chair from which he had half risen. "I really wouldn't miss your case for the world. It is most refreshingly unusual.

"But there is, if you will excuse my saying so, something just a little funny about it. What steps did you take when you found the card upon the door?"

"I was staggered, sir. I did not know what to do. Then I called at the offices nearby. But none of them seemed to know anything about it.

"Finally I went to the landlord, who is an accountant living on the ground floor. I asked him if he could tell me what had become of the Red-headed League. He said that he had never heard of any such group. Then I asked him who Mr. Duncan Ross was. He answered that the name was new to him.

" 'Well,' said I, 'the gentleman at No. 4.'

" 'What, the red-headed man?'

" 'Yes.'

" 'Oh,' said he, 'his name was William Morris. He was a lawyer. He was just using my room until his new offices were ready. He moved out yesterday.'

" 'Where could I find him?'

" 'Oh, at his new offices. He did tell me the address. Yes, 17 King Edward Street, near St. Paul's.'

"I started off, Mr. Holmes. But when I got to that address, it was a manufacturer of artificial kneecaps. No one in it had ever heard of either Mr. William Morris or Mr. Duncan Ross."

"And what did you do then?" asked Holmes.

"I went home to Saxe-Coburg Square and asked the advice of my assistant. But he could not help me in any way. He could only say that if I waited, I should hear by mail.

"But that was not quite good enough, Mr. Holmes. I did not wish to lose such a place without a struggle. And I had heard that you were good enough to give advice to poor folk who were in need of it. So I came right away to you."

"And you did very wisely," said Holmes. "Your case is a very remarkable one, and I shall be happy to look into it. From what you have told me, I think there may be something graver behind it than might first seem."

"Grave enough!" said Mr. Jabez Wilson. "Why, I have lost four pounds a week."

"As far as you are personally concerned," remarked Holmes, "I do not see that you have any complaint against this extraordinary league. On the contrary, I understand that you are richer by some thirty pounds. Moreover, you have gained detailed knowledge on every subject which comes under the letter A. You have lost nothing by them."

"No, sir. But I want to find out about them and who they are. I want to know what their object was in playing this prank—if it was a prank—upon me. It was a pretty expensive joke for them, for it cost them thirty-two pounds."

"We shall attempt to clear up these points for you. First, one or two questions, Mr. Wilson. This assistant of yours who first called your attention to the advertisement. How long had he been with you?"

"About a month then."

"How did he come?"

"In answer to an ad."

"Was he the only one who applied?"

"No, a dozen did."

"Why did you pick him?"

"Because he was handy and would come cheap."

"At half wages, in fact."

"Yes."

"What is he like, this Vincent Spaulding?"

"Small, stout, very quick in his ways, no hair on his face—though he's at least thirty. Has a white splash of acid upon his forehead."

Holmes sat up in his chair in great excitement. "I thought as much," said he. "Have you ever observed that his ears are pierced for earrings?''

"Yes, sir. He told me that a gypsy had done it for him when he was a lad.''

"Hum!" said Holmes, sinking back in deep thought. "He is still with you?''

"Oh, yes, sir. I have only just left him.''

"And has your business been attended to in your absence?''

"Nothing to complain about, sir. There's never very much to do in the mornings.''

"That will do, Mr. Wilson. I shall be happy to give you an opinion upon the subject after a day or two. Today is Saturday. I hope that by Monday we may come to a conclusion.''

"Well, Watson," said Holmes, when our visitor had left us, "what do you make of it all?''

"I make nothing of it," I answered, frankly. "It is a most mysterious business.''

"As a rule," said Holmes, "the more bizarre a thing is, the less mysterious it proves to be. A commonplace face is the most difficult to identify. In the same way, your commonplace, featureless crimes are really the most puzzling. But I must be prompt in this matter.''

"What are you going to do, then?'' I asked.

"To smoke," he answered. "It is quite a three-pipe problem. I beg that you won't speak to me for fifty minutes.''

He curled himself up in his chair, with his thin knees drawn up to his hawklike nose. There he sat with his eyes closed and his black clay pipe thrusting out like the bill of some strange bird.

I had come to the conclusion that he had dropped asleep. In fact, I was nodding myself. But then he suddenly sprang out of his chair with the gesture of a man who has made up his mind. He put his pipe down upon the mantelpiece.

"Sarasate plays at St. James's Hall this afternoon," he remarked. "What do you think, Watson? Could your patients spare you for a few hours?"

"I have nothing to do today. My practice is never very **absorbing**."

"Then put on your hat and come. I am going through the City first. We can have some lunch on the way. I see there is a good deal of German music on the program. That is rather more to my taste than Italian or French. It is **introspective**, and I want to introspect. Come along!"

We traveled by train as far as Aldersgate. A short walk took us to Saxe-Coburg Square, the scene of the odd story which we had listened to in the morning.

It was a poky, little, shabby-respectable place. Four lines of dingy, two-storied brick houses faced a small fenced-in park. There a lawn of weedy grass and a few clumps of faded bushes fought hard against unpleasant air heavy with smoke.

Three gold balls[7] and a brown board with JABEZ WILSON in white letters upon a corner house showed the place of our red-headed client's business. Sherlock Holmes stopped in front of it with his head on one side. He looked it all over, with his eyes shining brightly between puckered lids.

Then he walked slowly up the street and down again to the corner. He still looked keenly at the houses.

Finally he returned to the pawnbroker's. He thumped his stick hard on the pavement two or three times, then went up to the door and knocked. It was instantly opened by a bright-looking, clean-shaven young fellow. He asked him to step in.

"Thank you," said Holmes. "I only wished to ask how you would go from here to the Strand."

"Third right, fourth left," answered the assistant. He promptly closed the door.

"Smart fellow, that," observed Holmes as we walked

---

[7]Three gold balls are traditional symbols of a pawnbroker's shop.

away. "He is, in my judgment, the fourth smartest man in London. And for daring, he might even be considered third. I knew something about him before."

I said, "Evidently Mr. Wilson's assistant counts for a good deal in this mystery of the Red-headed League. I am sure that you asked your way merely in order to see him."

"Not him."

"What then?"

"The knees of his trousers."

"And what did you see?"

"What I expected to see."

"Why did you beat the pavement?"

"My dear doctor, this is a time for observation, not for talk. We are spies in an enemy's country. We know something of Saxe-Coburg Square. Let us now explore the parts which lie behind it."

The street we entered round the corner from sleepy Saxe-Coburg Square presented as great a contrast to it as the front of a picture does to the back. It was one of the main avenues which take the traffic of the City to the north and west. The roadway was blocked with an immense stream of vehicles flowing in and out. The pavements were black with the hurrying swarm of people.

We looked at the line of fine shops and stately businesses. It was difficult to realize that they really were directly behind the faded, **stagnant** square we had just left.

"Let me see," said Holmes. He stood at the corner and glanced along the street. "I want to remember the order of the houses here. It is a hobby of mine to have an exact knowledge of London. There is Mortimer's, the tobacco shop. Then the little newspaper shop, a branch of the City and Suburban Bank, the Vegetarian Restaurant, and McFarlane's carriage shop.

"That carries us right on to the other block. And now, doctor, we've done our work. It's time we had some play.

A sandwich and a cup of coffee.

"Then off to violinland, where all is sweetness, delicacy, and harmony. And no red-headed clients to annoy us with their puzzles."

My friend was an enthusiastic musician. He was himself not only a very capable performer but a composer of no ordinary skill.

All the afternoon he sat wrapped in the most perfect happiness, gently waving his long thin fingers in time to the music. His gently smiling face and his sleepy, dreamy eyes were very unlike those of the other Holmes. In fact, it was now impossible to imagine Holmes the detective hound; Holmes the relentless, keen-witted, ready-handed detective.

In his unique character, two aspects of his nature could be seen—now one, now the other. I have often thought that his extreme exactness and **astuteness** were a reaction against the poetic, thoughtful mood which sometimes ruled him. The swing of his nature took him from extreme laziness to devouring energy.

I knew that he was never so truly powerful as when he had been lounging in his armchair amid his music and books for days on end. Then it was that the lust of the chase would suddenly come upon him. Then his brilliant reasoning power would rise to the level of intuition. Those who were unfamiliar with his methods would look doubtfully on him. He began to seem to them a man whose knowledge was more than merely human.

I observed him that afternoon, wrapped up in the music. And I felt that an evil time might be coming for those whom he had set himself to hunt down.

"You want to go home, no doubt, doctor," he remarked, as we emerged.

"Yes, it would be as well."

"And I have some business to do which will take some hours. This business at Coburg Square is serious.

"A major crime is being planned. I have every reason to believe that we shall be in time to stop it. But today being Saturday rather complicates matters. I shall want your help tonight."

"At what time?"

"Ten will be early enough."

"I shall be at Baker Street at ten."

"Very well. And, I say, doctor! There may be some little danger. So kindly put your army revolver in your pocket."

He waved his hand, turned on his heel, and disappeared in an instant among the crowd.

I trust that I am not more dense than my neighbors. But I was always weighed down by a sense of my own stupidity in my dealing with Sherlock Holmes.

Here I had heard what he had heard. I had seen what he had seen. Yet from his words, it was evident that he saw clearly not only what had happened but what was about to happen. To me, the whole business was still confused and bizarre.

As I drove home to my house in Kensington I thought over it all. The extraordinary story of the red-headed copier of the *Encyclopaedia,* the visit to Saxe-Coburg Square, Holmes' last dark words. What did it all mean?

What was this night mission? Why should I go armed? Where were we going? And what were we to do?

I had the hint from Holmes that this smooth-faced assistant was a man to be reckoned with. He was a man who might play a deep game.

I tried to puzzle it out but gave it up in despair. I set the matter aside until night should bring an explanation.

It was a quarter-past nine when I started from home. I made my way across the park and so through Oxford Street to Baker Street. Two cabs were standing at the door.

As I entered the hallway, I heard the sound of voices from above. On entering his room, I found Holmes in lively conversation with two men.

One of them I recognized as Peter Jones, a police officer. The other was a tall, thin, sad-faced man. He wore a very shiny hat and a dreary, respectable coat.

"Ha! our party is complete," said Holmes. He buttoned up his pea jacket and took his heavy hunting stick from the rack.

"Watson, I think you know Mr. Jones of Scotland Yard? Let me introduce you to Mr. Merryweather. He will also be our companion in tonight's adventure."

"We're hunting in couples again, doctor, you see," said Jones. "Our friend here is a wonderful man for starting a chase. All he wants is an old dog to help him do the tracking down."

"I hope a wild goose may not prove to be the end of our chase," observed Mr. Merryweather gloomily.

"You may place great confidence in Mr. Holmes, sir," said the police agent in a superior tone. "He has his own little methods. If he won't mind my saying so, they are just a little too fantastic and rely too much on guesswork. But he has the makings of a detective in him.

"It is not too much to say that once or twice—as in the case of the Sholto murder and the Agra treasure—he has been more nearly correct than the police force."

"Oh, if you say so, Mr. Jones, it is all right!" said the stranger, with **deference**. "Still, I confess that I miss my game of cards. It is the first Saturday night in twenty-seven years that I have not had my game of cards."

"I think you will find," said Sherlock Holmes, "that you will play for a higher stake tonight than you have ever done yet.

"Moreover, you will find the play will be more exciting. For you, Mr. Merryweather, the stake will be some thirty thousand pounds. For you, Jones, it will be the man whom you wish to catch."

"John Clay: murderer, thief, smasher, and forger," said Mr. Jones. "He's a young man, Mr. Merryweather, but he is at the head of his profession. I would rather have my handcuffs on him than on any criminal in London.

"He's a remarkable man, is young John Clay. His grandfather was a royal duke. He himself has been to Eton and Oxford.[8]

"His brain is as cunning as his fingers. Though we find traces of him at every turn, we never know where to find the man himself. He'll rob a store in Scotland one week. The next he'll be raising money to build an orphanage in Cornwall. I've been on his track for years and have never set eyes on him yet."

"I hope that I may have the pleasure of introducing you tonight," said Holmes. "I've also had one or two little run-ins with Mr. John Clay. I agree with you that he is at the head of his profession.

"It is past ten, however, and quite time that we started. If you two will take the first cab, Watson and I will follow in the second."

Sherlock Holmes was not very talkative during the long drive. He lay back in the cab, humming the tunes which he had heard that afternoon. We rattled through an endless maze of gas-lit[9] streets until we emerged into Farringdon Street.

"We are nearly there now," my friend remarked. "This fellow Merryweather is a bank director and personally involved in the matter.

"I thought it well to have Jones with us also. He is not a bad fellow, though an absolute idiot in his job. He has one positive virtue. He is as brave as a bulldog and as **tenacious** as a lobster if he gets his claws upon anyone.

"Here we are, and they are waiting for us."

We had reached the same crowded street in which we had found ourselves that morning. Our cabs drove on. Follow-

---

[8]Oxford and Eton are highly respected English schools.

[9]During the time of the story, London street lamps were fueled by gas.

ing Mr. Merryweather's guidance, we passed down a narrow hall and through a side door which he opened for us.

Inside, there was a small corridor. At the end of that was a very heavy iron gate. This also was opened. It led down a flight of winding stone steps and **terminated** at another huge gate.

Mr. Merryweather stopped to light a lantern. Then he conducted us down a dark, earth-smelling passage. After opening a third door, he led us into a huge vault or cellar. This room was piled all round with crates and big boxes.

"You are not very **vulnerable** from above," Holmes remarked. He held up the lantern and gazed about him.

"Nor from below," said Mr. Merryweather. He struck his stick upon the stones which lined the floor.

"Why, dear me, it sounds quite hollow!" he remarked, looking up in surprise.

"I must really ask you to be a little more quiet," said Holmes severely. "You have already put the whole success of our mission at risk. Might I beg that you please sit down upon one of those boxes and not interfere?"

The solemn Mr. Merryweather perched himself upon a crate with a very injured expression upon his face. Meanwhile, Holmes fell to his knees upon the floor. With the lantern and a magnifying lens, he began to examine carefully the cracks between the stones.

A few seconds were enough to satisfy him. He sprang to his feet again and put his glass in his pocket.

"We have at least an hour before us," he remarked. "They can hardly take any steps until the good pawnbroker is safely in bed. Then they will not lose a minute. The sooner they do their work, the more time they will have for their escape.

"We are at present, doctor—as you have no doubt guessed—in the cellar of the City branch of one of the main London banks. Mr. Merryweather is the chairman of directors. He will explain to you why the more daring criminals of London should take a great interest in this cellar at present."

"It is our French gold," whispered the director. "We have had several warnings that an attempt might be made upon it."

"Your French gold?"

"Yes. Some months ago we wanted to strengthen our resources. For that purpose we borrowed thirty thousand napoleons[10] from the Bank of France.

"It has become known that we have never had time to unpack the money and that it is still lying in our cellar. The crate upon which I sit contains two thousand napoleons packed between layers of lead foil. Our gold supply is much larger at present than is usually kept in a single office. The directors have had **misgivings** upon the subject."

"Which were very well justified," observed Holmes. "And now it is time that we arranged our little plans. I expect that within an hour, matters will come to a head. In the meantime, Mr. Merryweather, we must put the shade over that lantern."

"And sit in the dark?"

"I am afraid so. I had brought a pack of cards in my pocket. I thought that, as there are four of us, you might have your game of cards after all.

"But I see that the enemy's preparations have gone so far that we cannot risk a light.

"So, first of all, we must choose our positions. These are daring men. Though we shall take them at a disadvantage, they may do us some harm unless we are careful.

"I shall stand behind this crate. You conceal yourself behind those. Then, when I flash a light upon them, close in swiftly. If they fire, Watson, do not hesitate to shoot them down."

I placed my revolver, cocked, upon the top of the wooden

---

[10]Napoleons are French gold coins.

case behind which I crouched. Holmes shot the slide across the front of his lantern. We were left in total darkness. It was a darkness more complete than any other I have ever experienced. The smell of hot metal remained to assure us that the light was still there, ready to flash out at a moment's notice.

My nerves were wound tight, ready for action. So to me, there was something depressing in the sudden gloom and in the cold, damp air.

"They have but one retreat," whispered Holmes. "That is back through the house into Saxe-Coburg Square. I hope that you have done what I asked you, Jones?"

"I have an inspector and two officers waiting at Wilson's front door."

"Then we have blocked all the holes. And now we must be silent and wait."

What a time it seemed! From comparing notes afterwards, it was but an hour and a quarter. Yet it seemed to me that the night must have almost passed and the dawn be breaking above us.

My limbs were weary and stiff, for I feared to change my position. Yet my nerves were worked up to the height of tension. And my hearing was so sharp that I could hear the gentle breathing of my companions. Indeed, I could tell the deeper, heavier breath of the bulky Jones from the thin, sighing note of the bank director.

From my position I could look over the case in the direction of the floor. Suddenly my eyes caught the glint of a light.

At first it was just a spark upon the stone pavement. Then it lengthened out until it became a yellow line. Without any warning or sound, a gash suddenly seemed to open.

A hand appeared—a white, almost womanly hand. It felt about in the center of the little area of light. For a minute or more the hand, with its moving fingers, stuck out of the floor. Then it was withdrawn as suddenly as it appeared. All was dark again except for the single spark which marked a gap between the stones.

However, it disappeared for just a moment. With a ripping, tearing sound, one of the broad white stones turned over upon its side. A square hole was left, through which streamed the light of a lantern.

Over the edge there peeped a clean-cut, boyish face, which looked keenly about. With a hand on either side of the hole, the man drew himself shoulder-high, then waist-high. Finally he stopped with one knee resting on the edge.

In another instant he stood at the side of the hole. He began hauling after him a companion. This fellow was lean and small like himself. He had a pale face and a head of very red hair.

"It's all clear," he whispered. "Have you the chisel and the bags? Great Scot! Jump, Archie, jump, and I'll swing for it!"

Sherlock Holmes had sprung out and seized the intruder by the collar. The other dived down the hole. I heard the sound of tearing cloth as Jones clutched at his coat. The light flashed upon the barrel of a revolver. But Holmes' hunting stick came down on the man's wrist. The pistol clinked upon the stone floor.

"It's no use, John Clay," said Holmes, calmly. "You have no chance at all."

"So I see," the other answered with the greatest coolness. "I imagine that my pal is all right, though I see you have got his coattails."

"There are three men waiting for him at the door," said Holmes.

"Oh, indeed. You seem to have done the thing very completely. I must compliment you."

"And I you," Holmes answered. "Your red-headed idea was very new and effective."

"You'll see your pal again presently," said Jones. "He's quicker at climbing down holes than I am. Just hold out your hands while I fix the cuffs."

"I beg that you will not touch me with your filthy hands," remarked our prisoner as the handcuffs clattered upon his wrists. "You may not be aware that I have royal blood in my veins. Have the goodness also, when you address me, always to say 'sir' and 'please.' "

"All right," said Jones with a stare and a snicker. "Well, would you please, sir, march upstairs. There we can get a cab to carry your highness to the police station."

"That is better," said John Clay, **serenely**. He made a sweeping bow to the three of us. Then he walked quietly off with the detective.

"Really, Mr. Holmes," said Mr. Merryweather as we followed them, "I do not know how the bank can thank you or repay you. You have discovered and defeated one of the most determined bank robberies I have ever known."

"I have had one or two little scores of my own to settle with Mr. John Clay," said Holmes. "I have had a few small expenses because of this matter. I shall expect the bank to refund that amount.

"But beyond that, I am well repaid. I have had an experience which is in many ways unique. And I have heard the very remarkable story of the Red-headed League."

Later, back at Baker Street, Holmes explained the case to me in the early hours of the morning. We sat enjoying a glass of whisky and soda.

Holmes began, "You see, Watson, it was perfectly obvious from the first. There was only one possible object of this rather odd ad for the League and the copying of the *Encyclopaedia*. Someone wanted to get this not overbright pawnbroker out of the way for a few hours every day.

"It was a curious way of managing it. But, really, it would be difficult to suggest a better. The method was no doubt suggested to Clay's clever mind by the color of his partner's hair. The four pounds a week was the bait which must draw him. And what did four pounds matter to them? They were playing for thousands.

"So they put the ad in the paper. One **rogue** has the temporary office. The other rogue urges Wilson to apply for the job. Together they manage to make sure he is out of his shop every morning in the week.

"From the time that I heard of the assistant having accepted half wages, it was obvious to me that he had some strong motive for taking the job."

"But how could you guess what the motive was?"

"Had there been women in the house, I should have suspected a mere vulgar affair. That, however, was out of the question.

"The man's business was a small one. So there was nothing in the house which could account for such elaborate preparations and such expenses as theirs.

"It must then be something outside the house. What could it be? I thought of the assistant's fondness for photography and his trick of vanishing into the cellar. The cellar! There was the end of this tangled clue.

"Then I asked some questions about this mysterious assistant. I found that I had to deal with one of the coolest and most daring criminals in London.

"He was doing something in the cellar—something which took many hours a day for months on end.

"What could it be, I asked myself again? I could think of nothing except that he was running a tunnel to some other building.

"I had concluded that much when we went to visit the scene of action. I surprised you by beating upon the pavement with my stick. I was determining whether the cellar stretched out in front or behind. It was not in front.

"Then I rang the bell. As I hoped, the assistant answered

it. We have had some run-ins, but we had never set eyes upon each other before.

"I hardly looked at his face. His knees were what I wished to see. You must yourself have remarked how worn, wrinkled, and stained they were. They spoke of those hours of digging.

"The only remaining point was what they were digging for. I walked round the corner. There I saw the City and Suburban Bank at the back of our friend's business. I then felt that I had solved my problem.

"When you drove home after the concert, I called upon Scotland Yard[11] and the chairman of the bank directors. You have seen the results."

"And how could you tell they would make their attempt tonight?" I asked.

"Well, when they closed their League offices, that was a sign that they no longer cared about Mr. Jabez Wilson's presence. In other words, they had completed their tunnel.

"But they had to use it soon since it might be discovered or the gold might be removed. Saturday would suit them better than any other day. It would give them two days for their escape. For all these reasons I expected them to come tonight."

"You reasoned it out beautifully," I exclaimed in genuine admiration. "It is so long a chain. Yet every link rings true."

"It saved me from boredom," he answered, yawning. "Alas! I already feel it closing in upon me. My life is spent in one long effort to escape from the commonplaces of existence. These little problems help me to do so."

"And you are a benefactor of the race," said I.

He shrugged his shoulders. "Well, perhaps, after all, it is of some little use," he remarked. " *'L'homme c'est rien— l'oeuvre c'est tout,'* as Gustave Flaubert wrote to George Sand."[12]

---

[11]Scotland Yard is the site of London police headquarters.

[12]This French phrase means, "The man is nothing—the work is everything." Flaubert (1821-1880) and Sand (1804-1876) were French writers.

"The Red-headed League" was first published in 1891.

INSIGHTS INTO
ARTHUR CONAN DOYLE

(1859-1930)

Doyle was a natural storyteller all his life. His first tale was a horror story about a man who was eaten alive by a tiger. He completed this story when he was six.

Later, at boarding school, Doyle spun more tales for his classmates. He knew how to play his audience too. He always threatened to end his tale at the most exciting moment. Then he would demand a jam tart or an apple from his listeners before he would finish the story.

Doyle began to study medicine at Edinburgh University in 1877. One of his professors there was Dr. Joseph Bell. Bell was a thin, sharp-nosed man who could instantly guess most of his patients' illnesses. He also loved to figure out other facts about his patients just by noting small details.

For instance, Dr. Bell once announced to his class that a patient was "a left-handed cobbler." He explained to his puzzled students, "You'll observe, gentlemen, the worn places on the trousers where a cobbler rests his lapstone? The right-hand side, you'll note, is far more worn than the left. He uses his left hand for hammering the leather."

Then Bell added, with a note of glee, "The trained eye! A simple matter."

Doyle soon became Dr. Bell's clerk. And Bell later served as the model for the thin, hawk-nosed, amazingly sharp Sherlock Holmes.

continued

Sports were always an important part of Doyle's life. As a youngster, he enjoyed cricket, boxing, swimming, and rugby. Later he eagerly tried golfing, skiing, cycling, and even race car driving.

Once, during a visit to Switzerland, Doyle wanted to ski. At that time no one in the country skied. But a sporting goods store owner agreed to order equipment from Norway.

When the gear came, Doyle, the store owner, and the owner's brother strapped on the skis and started off. As they glided into a village at the end of their run, they were greeted by an amazed crowd and ringing bells. Doyle predicted—correctly, of course—that skiing would become one of Switzerland's most popular sports.

Though he practiced medicine for several years, Doyle was never a very successful doctor.

One year Doyle's tax form was returned because he did not fill it out right. The tax inspector had written across the form, "Most unsatisfactory."

Doyle scribbled the words "I entirely agree" and mailed it back in. But Doyle wasn't making an apology. He was referring to the small amount of income recorded on the form.

Sherlock Holmes was and is one of the most popular story characters of all time. Some readers actually believed the detective was a real person. In fact, Doyle received many letters addressed to Holmes.

When Holmes retired in one story, several women wrote applying to be his housekeeper. The reaction to Holmes' death in another story was even more dramatic. Readers in London wore mourning clothes for days. Doyle was finally pressured into bringing the detective back from the grave.

In short, Holmes became so famous that he overshadowed his creator. This fact often annoyed Doyle. Once, when someone continued to call him "Sir Sherlock Holmes," Doyle refused to answer. When pressed, he finally roared, "My name, sir, is Conan Doyle!"

Other works by Doyle:
"The Adventure of the Dancing Men," short story
"The Adventure of the Speckled Band," short story
"The Final Problem," short story
"The Five Orange Pips," short story
"The Musgrave Ritual," short story
"A Scandal in Bohemia," short story
The Hound of the Baskervilles, novel
The Lost World, novel
A Study in Scarlet, novel

THE OPEN WINDOW

SAKI

VOCABULARY PREVIEW

Below is a list of words that appear in the story. Read the list and get to know the words before you start the story.

absence—lack; state of being missing
ailments—diseases; sicknesses
communion—fellowship
comprehension—understanding
convey—communicate; transmit
discounting—ignoring; overlooking
endeavored—tried
engulfed—drowned; swallowed up
ghastly—gruesome or horrifying
habitation—the act of living in a place
headlong—hasty; rushing
imminent—about to occur; approaching
infirmities—frailties; weaknesses (especially physical)
migrate—move
moping—sulking or brooding
scarcity—shortage; undersupply
self-possessed—calm and collected
shudder—shiver; shake
succession—chain or series
treacherous—risky; tricky in a dangerous way

THE OPEN WINDOW

A quiet rest in the country is what Framton Nuttel needs. After a few visits to the neighbors, he hopes to settle down to a peaceful life.

Little does Nuttel know that things are always stirring in the country. Even things from beyond the grave.

"My aunt will be down soon, Mr. Nuttel," said a very **self-possessed** young lady of fifteen. "In the meantime, you must try and put up with me."

Framton Nuttel **endeavored** to say the correct something which would flatter the niece, his present company. At the same time he wanted to avoid **discounting** the aunt soon to appear.

SAKI

Privately he doubted more than ever if these formal visits to a **succession** of total strangers would help the nerve cure which he was supposed to be undergoing.

"I know how it will be," his sister had said when he was preparing to **migrate** to this country retreat. "You will bury yourself down there and not speak to a living soul. Your nerves will be worse than ever from **moping**.

"I shall just give you letters to introduce you to all the people I know there. Some of them, as far as I can remember, were quite nice."

Framton wondered if Mrs. Sappleton, the lady to whom he was presenting one of the letters, came into the nice category.

"Do you know many of the people round here?" asked the niece, when she judged that their silent **communion** had lasted long enough.

"Hardly a soul," said Framton. "My sister stayed here at the rectory,[1] you know, some four years ago. She gave me letters to introduce me to some of the people here."

He made the last statement in a tone of distinct regret.

"Then you know practically nothing about my aunt?" pursued the self-possessed young lady.

"Only her name and address," admitted the caller. He was wondering whether Mrs. Sappleton was in the married or widowed state. Something undefinable about the room suggested male **habitation**.

"Her great tragedy happened just three years ago," said the child. "That would have been after your sister left."

"Her tragedy?" asked Framton. Somehow in this restful country spot tragedies seemed out of place.

"You may wonder why we keep that window wide open on an October afternoon," said the niece. She gestured to a large French window[2] that opened onto a lawn.

"It is quite warm for this time of the year," said Framton. "But has that window got anything to do with the tragedy?"

---

[1]A rectory is a clergyman's house.
[2]A French window extends from floor to ceiling and opens like a door.

"Out through that window, three years ago today, her husband and her two young brothers went off for their day's shooting. They never came back. In crossing the moor[3] to their favorite hunting ground, they were all three **engulfed** in a **treacherous** marsh.

"It had been that dreadful wet summer, you know. Places that were safe in other years suddenly gave way without warning.

"Their bodies were never recovered. That was the dreadful part of it."

Here the child's voice lost its self-possessed note and became touchingly hesitant. "Poor aunt always thinks that they will come back some day, they and the little brown spaniel that was lost with them. She imagines they will walk in at that window just as they used to do. That is why it is kept open every evening till it is dusk.

"Poor dear aunt. She has often told me how they went out, her husband with his white waterproof coat over his arm. And Ronnie, her youngest brother, singing, 'Bertie, why do you bound?' He always did that to tease her because she said it got on her nerves.

"Do you know, sometimes on still, quiet evenings like this, I almost get a creepy feeling. I begin to feel that they will all walk in through that window—"

She broke off with a little **shudder**. It was a relief to Framton when the aunt bustled into the room with a whirl of apologies for being late.

"I hope Vera has been amusing you?" she said.

"She has been very interesting," said Framton.

"I hope you don't mind the open window," said Mrs. Sappleton briskly. "My husband and brothers will be home soon from shooting. They always come in this way. They've been out hunting in the marshes today. They'll undoubtedly make a fine mess of my poor carpets. So like you menfolk, isn't it?"

---

[3]A moor is an area of open, often marshy land.

She rattled on cheerfully about the shooting, the **scarcity** of birds, and the outlook for duck in the winter.

To Framton it was all purely horrible. He made a desperate but only half successful effort to turn the talk to a less **ghastly** topic.

He was conscious that his hostess was giving him only part of her attention. Her eyes were constantly straying past him to the open window and the lawn. It was certainly an unlucky coincidence that he should have paid his visit on this tragic anniversary.

"The doctors agree that I must have complete rest. They've also ordered the **absence** of all mental excitement and any violent physical exercise," announced Framton.

He was a victim of a rather common delusion. Such people think that total strangers and chance acquaintances hunger for the least detail of one's **ailments** and **infirmities**, their cause and cure.

"On the matter of diet they are not so much in agreement," he continued.

"No?" said Mrs. Sappleton. Only at the last moment did she manage to cover a yawn.

Then she suddenly brightened into alert attention—but not to what Framton was saying.

"Here they are at last!" she cried. "Just in time for tea. Don't they look as if they were muddy up to the eyes!"

Framton shivered slightly. He turned towards the niece with a look meant to **convey** sympathetic **comprehension**.

The child was staring out through the open window with dazed horror in her eyes. In a chill shock of nameless fear, Framton swung round in his seat and looked in the same direction.

In the deepening twilight three figures were walking across the lawn towards the window. They all carried guns under their arms. One of them had the added burden of a white coat, which hung over his shoulders. A tired brown spaniel kept close to their heels.

Noiselessly they neared the house. Then a hoarse young voice chanted out of the dusk, "I said, Bertie, why do you bound?"

Framton grabbed wildly at his stick and hat. He only dimly noted the hall door, the gravel drive, and the front gate in his **headlong** retreat. A cyclist coming along the road had to run into the bushes to avoid an **imminent** crash.

"Here we are, my dear," said the man with the white overcoat as he came in through the window. "Fairly muddy, but most of it's dry. Who was that who bolted out as we came up?"

"A most extraordinary man, a Mr. Nuttel," said Mrs. Sappleton. "Could only talk about his illness. Then he dashed off without a word of goodbye or apology when you arrived. One would think he had seen a ghost."

"I expect it was the spaniel," said the niece calmly. "He told me he had a horror of dogs. He was once hunted into a cemetery somewhere on the banks of the Ganges[4] by a pack of wild dogs.

"He had to slip down into a newly-dug grave. All night the creatures stood snarling and grinning and foaming just above him. Enough to make any one lose their nerve."

Romance at short notice was her specialty.

[4]The Ganges is a river in India.

"The Open Window" was first published in 1914.

INSIGHTS INTO SAKI

(1870-1916)

Saki (or Hector Hugh Munro) spent his childhood in a huge eighteenth-century home.

But the house could seem crowded at times. Living with Saki were his brother, sister, two aunts, and grandmother.

Apart from immediate family, servants, governesses, a gardener, and the family doctor also lived there. And for extra company, the family kept tortoises, rabbits, doves, guinea pigs, cats, and poultry.

Saki's mother died while he was just a baby. His father left the children in the care of his two maiden aunts.

These aunts were not the best candidates for the job. They argued constantly and were overly strict. They kept the children indoors most of the time. This explains why Saki turned to books for entertainment.

Those years were not quickly forgotten by Saki. He reflected his loveless, harsh childhood in two of his best-known stories: "The Lumber Room" and "Sredni Vashtar."

Saki was known to be highly perceptive and intelligent. The quick-witted writer could not stand anyone whom he considered dull or stupid. His distaste for those boring and clumsy souls is obvious in "The Sheep."

Even after he was published, Saki found he could not support himself by just writing books. He realized he would have to become a journalist if he seriously wanted to earn a living as a writer.

But Saki hated this work. He even hated dressing like other journalists. He rebelled against his position by always wearing a high-society bowler hat.

Saki later balanced his hatred of journalism with his upper-class attitudes by working at London's *Morning Post*. This newspaper had the virtue for Saki of being read by the upper class.

Saki had painstaking writing habits. He would go over every sentence and decide if each word reflected exactly what he meant. Sometimes he would try every possible word—whether it was two or twenty—before deciding upon the perfect one.

It was once said that Saki "chose his words as the last of the dandies might choose his ties."

Saki romanticized war and enlisted quite eagerly. He wrote, "It seems almost too good to be true that I am going to take an active part in a big European war [WWI]."

He was so determined to fight on the front that again and again he refused offers of a safer position.

One of these offers even came from a general. While the general was walking in the trenches, he recognized Saki from a dinner party in London. He offered Saki a job far from the fighting.

But Saki excused himself. He said it had taken him two years to reach the front and that he desired to remain there.

Saki was killed shortly afterwards by an enemy bullet. His last words were, "Put out that bloody cigarette."

Other works by Saki:
"Gabriel-Ernest," short story
"Hyacinth," short story
"The Interlopers," short story
"The Story-Teller," short story
"Tobermory," short story
"The Unrest Cure," short story
The Unbearable Bassington, novel
The Watched Pot, play

THE PARDONER'S TALE

GEOFFREY CHAUCER

VOCABULARY PREVIEW

Below is a list of words that appear in the story. Read the list and get to know the words before you start the story.

abominable—horrible and hateful
absolve—to free from guilt, obligation, or blame
adversary—enemy or opponent
amend—improve or correct
assent—agreement; consent
avarice—greed for money and gain
blithe—lighthearted; merry
brethren—brothers
felicity—great happiness
gluttony—piggishness; the habit of eating too much
grisly—hideous and disgusting
habitation—dwelling; where one lives
hoard—stockpile of valued objects
kindle—light; set afire
plighted—pledged
sacrament—sacred religious ritual
tarry—delay; wait
trespass—to offend or sin
vermin—annoying, destructive creatures, such as rats or roaches; pests
visage—face

◆ T H E ◆

PARDONER'S
TALE ◆ GEOFFREY ◆ CHAUCER

◆ ━━━━━━━━━━━━━━━━━━━━━━━ ◆

The trip to Canterbury was a favorite religious pilgrimage for folk in medieval England.[1] Chaucer wrote about one such pilgrim group in his *Canterbury Tales*. The tales are those told by Chaucer's colorful characters to pass the time on the road.

When the Pardoner's[2] turn comes, he offers a story about three rash gamblers who find a grand treasure. But these riches come at a price. Both Death and the Devil will have their due.

There once lived in Flanders[3] a company of young folk who devoted themselves to folly. They lived riotous lives and gambled. They visited houses of prostitution and taverns. There, with harps, lutes, and guitars, they danced and threw the dice day and night. They ate and drank much more than they could handle, too.

[1]Canterbury Cathedral was considered holy because St. Thomas á Becket was murdered there in 1170. Becket, who defended the rights of the church against the state, was killed by King Henry II's men.

[2]A pardoner was a man given the right by the pope to sell pardons for sins. Pardoners did not have to be members of a holy order.

[3]Flanders was a wealthy, independent country in northern Europe during the Middle Ages.

Thus they served the Devil in those temples of the Devil in cursed fashion and with **abominable** excesses. Their curses were so violent and damnable that it was **grisly** to hear them swear. They tore our blessed Lord's body in pieces all over again.[4] They acted as if the Jews had not tortured him enough! And each laughed at the others' sins.

And then came dancing girls and graceful and slim young women carrying fruit. Singers with harps, pimps, and sellers of sweets followed.

All these people were the servants of the Devil. They were ready to **kindle** and blow the fire of lust that is closely linked to **gluttony**. I take the Holy Bible as my witness that sin is in wine and drunkenness. . . .

These three rioters of which I tell had sat down in a tavern to drink long before the morning bell struck nine o'clock. And as they sat, they heard a bell clang. The bell was ringing for a corpse that was being carried to his grave.

Then one of them called to his servant. "Go," he said, "and ask quickly whose corpse this is passing by here. And be sure that you get his name right."

"Sir," said the young servant, "that isn't at all necessary. I was told, two hours before you came, that he was an old friend of yours. He was suddenly slain last night as he sat on his bench, very drunk.

"There came a secret thief men call Death," the servant continued. "In his country all the people sleep. With his spear, he split your friend's heart in two. Then he went his way without another word. He has slain a thousand with this plague.[5]

"And, master, before you come into his presence, I think it would wise to be warned about such an **adversary**. Always be ready to meet him. My mother taught me this. I'll say no more."

---

[4]The rioters are "tearing apart" Christ by using oaths such as "by God's bones." (The passage also reveals a typical medieval prejudice against Jews.)

[5]A plague is a deadly disease that kills many people in a short time. The Black Death, a terrible plague, struck Europe during the fourteenth century.

The tavernkeeper said, "By Saint Mary, this child speaks the truth. In a big village a mile from here, Death has slain this year every man, woman, child, worker, and servant. I believe that must be his **habitation**. It would be very wise to be warned about Death before he attacks you."

"Yes, by God's arms," said one rioter. "Is it so dangerous to meet up with him? I shall seek him by every path and street. I make this promise on God's worthy bones!

"Listen, fellows," he said, looking at his friends. "We three are all of one mind. Let each of us give his hand to the other two and become brothers. We will slay this false traitor Death. By God's honor, before night falls, he shall be slain who has slain so many."

Together these three **plighted** their word to live and die for each other as though they were all brothers. Then up they got, all drunk and in a rage. They went toward that village which the tavernkeeper had spoken of before.

And many a grisly oath they swore and tore Christ's blessed body. They declared that Death should indeed die if they could just catch him!

They had gone nearly half a mile. Just as they were about to cross a stile,[6] they met an old, poor man.

This old man greeted them very meekly and said, "Now, lords, God be with you!"

The proudest of the three rioters answered, "What? Bad luck to you, fellow! Why are you all wrapped up except for your face? Why have you lived so long and grown so old?"

The old man peered into the other's **visage**. He said, "Because, though I have walked to India, I cannot find a man in city or village who will change his youth for my age. And, therefore, I must keep my age as long as it is God's will. No, alas, not even Death will take my life!

"Thus I walk," the old man complained, "like a restless prisoner. And I knock with my staff on the ground, which is my mother's gate. Both morning and night, I knock and

---

[6]A stile is a short staircase built over a fence.

say, 'Dear mother, let me in! See how I'm fading—flesh, blood, and skin! Alas, when shall my bones be at rest?

" 'Mother, I would exchange with you my chest that has been in my chamber a long time. Yes, I would even trade it for a hairshirt.'[7]

"But yet she will not do me that favor. That is why my face is so pale and wrinkled.

"But, sirs, it is not courteous to insult an old man unless he **trespass** against you in words or deeds. You may well read for yourself in the Holy Book: 'You should rise up and honor an old man with white hair.'

"Therefore, I'll give you good advice. Never harm an old man—no more than you would like men to harm you when you are old, if you live so long.

"Now God be with you, where you walk or ride. I must go where I have to go."

"No, old fellow. By God, you shall not," said this other gambler at once. "You don't get off as lightly as that, by Saint John!

"You spoke just now of this traitor Death, who slays all our friends hereabout. Now I swear, you are his spy. Tell us where he is or you shall pay for it, by God and the holy **sacrament**! For I'm sure you're in on his plan to slay us young folk, you false thief!"

"Now, sirs," the old man said, "if you are so eager to find Death, turn up this crooked path. I swear to you that I left him there in that grove, under a tree. There he will wait. He will not hide, despite your boasting.

"Do you see that oak? Right there you shall find him. God, who saved all mankind, save you and **amend** you." This is what the old man said.

The three rioters ran until they reached that tree. There they found fine gold-crowned florins.[8] There were almost eight bushels, they thought.

---

[7]Since a hairshirt is scratchy, it usually was worn by sinners to punish themselves. Here, the old man thinks of such a shirt as his burial clothes.

[8]A florin is a Dutch coin.

No longer then did they seek Death. Each of them was so gladdened by the sight—because the florins were so bright and fair—that they sat down by the precious **hoard**.

The worst of the three spoke the first word. "**Brethren**," he said, "listen to what I say. I am very smart, though I joke and party. Fortune has given us this treasure so that we may live our lives in mirth and happiness. And as easily as it came to us, so will we spend it.

"Eh! God's precious honor! Who supposed today that our luck should be so good? If we just might carry this gold from here to my house or else to one of yours, then we'd be at the height of **felicity**. For you know full well that this gold is ours.

"But truly we can't do it by day. Men would say that we were strong thieves and hang us on account of our treasure.

"This treasure must be carried away by night, as wisely and cleverly as we can manage it. Therefore, I advise that we draw lots. Let us see where the shortest stick will fall. And he that draws the short stick shall run to town with a **blithe** heart and with all due speed. He shall secretly bring us back bread and wine.

"The other two of us shall cunningly guard this treasure. And when night comes—if it does not keep us waiting—we will carry this treasure wherever we think is best. We will all **assent** to the choice."

Then one of them gathered the sticks in his fist. He told them to draw and see where the short stick would fall. And it fell on the youngest of the three. So he went at once to town.

As soon as he was gone, one of them spoke to the other. "You well know that you are my sworn brother. Now I'll tell you something of profit to you.

"You see that our partner is gone. Here is the gold—and heaps of it—that shall be divided among us three.

"But suppose I could fix it so that it would be divided

among just us two? Wouldn't I have proved myself your friend?''

The other answered, "I don't know how that can be. He knows the gold is with us two. What shall we do? What shall we say to him?''

"Shall it be a secret?" said the first villain. "If so, I will tell you in a few words what we shall do to bring it about.''

"I agree," said the other. "I will not betray you. I swear it.''

"Now," said the first, "you know that there are two of us. Two shall be stronger than one. Look here, after he has sat down, get up and act as though you wanted to wrestle with him. And while you are struggling with him as though in sport, I shall run him clean through the side. You do the same with your dagger.

"Then all his gold shall be divided between you and me, my dear friend. So we both will fulfill all our desires and play at dice whenever we want.''

Thus the two villains agreed to murder the third, as you have heard me say.

The youngest, who went to town, often turned over in his mind the beauty of those new, bright florins. "Oh Lord!" he said. "If only I could have this treasure all to myself! Then there would be no man under the throne of God who should live as merrily as I!''

At last the Fiend, our enemy, put it into his mind that he should buy poison to slay his partners. You see, the young man had such bad desires that the Fiend was allowed to tempt him to damnation. It was the young man's full intention to slay both of his partners and never to regret it.

So he would not **tarry** any longer. On he went into town, to a druggist. He asked the druggist to sell him some poison, so he might kill rats.

He said there was also a polecat[9] in his yard who had slain his chickens. He wanted revenge, if he could, on the

---

[9]A polecat is a ferretlike animal found in Europe.

vermin that destroyed him by night.

The druggist answered, "May God save my soul, I'll give you such a thing. In all this world, no creature can eat or drink of this mixture without dying at once. Even if just a drop the size of a grain of wheat is taken, it will work.

"Yes, he who takes it shall die and in less time than it takes to walk a mile. This poison is that strong and violent."

The cursed young man took the box of poison in his hand. Then he ran into the next street to another man and borrowed from him three large bottles. He poured poison into two of these. The third he kept clean for his drink. He planned to work all night, carrying the gold out of that place.

And when this rioter—heading for hell—had filled his three big bottles, he returned to his friends.

Why make a sermon of it? Just as they had planned his death before, the two quickly murdered the youngest.

When this was done, one of them said, "Now let us sit and drink and make merry. Afterward, we will bury his body."

With that, he happened to pick up a bottle with poison in it. He drank, as did his partner. Thereupon they both died.

* * * * *

Now, good men, God forgive you your trespasses.[10] And guard yourselves from **avarice**. My holy pardon may cure you all—if you offer coins or silver brooches, spoons, and rings. Bow your head before this holy document I have here.

Come up, you wives. Offer your wool. I will enter your names on my roll and you shall go to the bliss of heaven. I will **absolve** you by my high power—you who will make an offering. I will leave you as clean and clear as when you were born. . . .

It is an honor to everyone here to have a pardoner to absolve you as you ride through the country. Accidents may

---

[10]The Pardoner is addressing the other pilgrims in his group.

happen. Perhaps one or two of you may fall down off his horse and break his neck in two.

See what a blessing it is to you all that I have fallen into your company. I can absolve you, both great and lowly, when the soul shall pass from the body.

Copies of "The Pardoner's Tale" probably first appeared during Chaucer's life in the 1390s. When the printing press was introduced to England, Chaucer's work was among the first printed.

INSIGHTS INTO
GEOFFREY CHAUCER

(1340-1400)

Chaucer's great love of books is expressed in many of his poems. His works also show that he was very well read.

Some historians believe that Chaucer owned as many as sixty books. In the fourteenth century, books were rare and valuable. A personal library of sixty books would have been enormous.

Chaucer was the son of a middle-class wine merchant. But one of his closest friends was a prince.

John of Gaunt, son of King Edward III, probably met Chaucer when both men were seventeen. They became life-long friends.

Chaucer's first great poem was written to honor Gaunt's wife after her death. This poem was called the *Book of the Duchess*.

Gaunt later married again. His second wife, Katherine Swynford, was the sister of Chaucer's wife. Thus the two men ended up not only friends but brothers-in-law.

Chaucer married Philippa Roet in September 1366. Their first child, Elizabeth, was born nine months later.

Some experts think Elizabeth was really John of Gaunt's child. They believe Gaunt may have paid Chaucer to marry Philippa. These scholars point out that Gaunt gave a large sum to the couple when Chaucer married Philippa. Gaunt continued to be very generous to both Philippa and Elizabeth for the rest of their lives.

The Chaucers probably had two more children, Thomas and Lewis. It is possible Thomas was also Gaunt's child.

continued

But many people deny the rumor, pointing out that Chaucer seemed a loving husband and father. So the subject remains a mystery.

Another mystery in Chaucer's life occurred in the year 1380. Court records tell us that Chaucer was cleared on a charge of *raptus*. *Raptus* is a Latin word that means either rape or kidnapping.

Most who have studied Chaucer's life do not believe the gentle poet could have been guilty of either crime. In any case, the charges against him were dropped.

In medieval times, scientists called *alchemists* tried to change metals into gold. Chaucer seems to have at least known something about the topic. He mentions it in the "Second Nun's Tale" and the "Canon's Yeoman's Tale." In fact, for several hundred years after his death, some thought Chaucer was a secret master of alchemy.

Records show that Chaucer often borrowed money late in his life. Some historians believe Chaucer may have needed extra funds because he was investing—and losing—money with alchemists.

Throughout his life, Chaucer received many gifts from King Edward III and his sons. He was given yearly pensions and cash gifts. At one time he was granted a pitcher of wine daily for the rest of his life.

But perhaps the loveliest gift Chaucer received came from Gaunt's son, King Henry IV. He gave Chaucer a beautiful fur-trimmed red robe. It cost well over eight pounds. That comes to more than $2,000 in today's terms.

King Edward III may not have valued Chaucer as highly as his grandson, Henry IV, did. Early in 1360, Chaucer was serving in the King's army when he was captured in France. The King paid sixteen pounds ($3,840) to ransom Chaucer. About the same time, the King paid twenty pounds ($4,800) for a warhorse!

Of course, in 1360, Chaucer had not yet gained fame as a poet. The King was simply paying what he thought a good soldier was worth.

Tradition holds that Chaucer studied law for a time. The author did sign some documents as "attorney." Chaucer's writings also show that he understood far more of the law than the common person would have.

Most scholars believe Chaucer studied law at a school in London called the Inner Temple. Temple records show that a "Geffrye Chaucer" was once fined for beating a friar.

Is the Chaucer in the records Chaucer the author? No one knows. And no one knows Chaucer the author's view of friars. But the one friar he did create in *The Canterbury Tales* is lustful, greedy, and dishonest.

Other works by Chaucer:
   "The Knight's Tale,"
   "The Miller's Tale,"   } all from
   "The Nun's Priest's Tale,"   } *The Canterbury Tales*
   "The Wife of Bath's Tale,"

The House of Fame, poetry
The Parliament of Fowls, poetry
Troilus and Criseide, poetry

THE ADVENTURE OF
THE SPECKLED BAND

ARTHUR CONAN DOYLE

VOCABULARY PREVIEW

Below is a list of words that appear in the story. Read the list and get to know the words before you start the story.

agitation—state of being disturbed, excited, or troubled
aristocratic—of noble blood; upperclass
averse—unwilling; reluctant
blandly—smoothly and gently
compliance—behavior that conforms to a request or order; obedience
comprehensive—complete; overall
dawdling—delaying; lagging
deductions—conclusions reached by reasoning
deprived—took something away from; stripped or robbed
extinguished—blown or blotted out
gaping—opened wide
impending—about to occur; upcoming
perplexity—puzzlement
pittance—small and skimpy amount
pretense—false excuse or action, meant to deceive
prolong—lengthen or stretch out
protruding—sticking out
scruple—feeling of doubt about whether an action is right or wrong
vigil—a period during which one keeps watch
writhed—twisted and squirmed

THE SPECKLED BAND

ARTHUR CONAN DOYLE

Something deadly is stalking the residents of Stoke Moran. Outside the manor house, a cheetah and baboon roam the grounds. Inside is Dr. Roylott, a man of dangerous temper and strength.

One bizarre death has already occurred. The stage is set for a second. Master detective Sherlock Holmes can solve the case only by finding the mysterious speckled band.

During the last eight years, I have studied some seventy or so cases of my friend Sherlock Holmes. On glancing over my notes about these cases, I find many tragic, some comic, and a large number merely strange. But none have been commonplace.

Holmes worked for the love of his art rather than for wealth. So he refused any investigation which did not tend to be unusual and even fantastic.

Yet of all these cases, I cannot recall any more strange than that concerning the well-known Surrey family, the Roylotts of Stoke Moran.

The events in question occurred in the early days of my friendship with Holmes. We were still sharing rooms as bachelors on Baker Street at the time.

I probably would have recorded these events before now. But I promised secrecy at the time. I have only been freed from this promise during the last month by the untimely death of the lady to whom the pledge was given.

It is perhaps as well that the facts should now come to light. I have reason to know that there are widespread rumors about the death of Dr. Grimesby Roylott. These rumors have tended to make the matter even more terrible than the truth.

It was early in April in the year 1883 that our adventure began. I woke one morning to find Sherlock Holmes standing, fully dressed, by the side of my bed.

He was a late riser as a rule. But the clock on the mantelpiece showed me that it was only a quarter past seven. So I blinked up at him in some surprise and perhaps just a little resentment. You see, I myself was regular in my habits.

"Very sorry to disturb you, Watson," he said. "I'm afraid it's the common lot this morning. Mrs. Hudson has been disturbed, she disturbed me, and I you."

"What is it then—a fire?"

"No, a client. It seems that a young lady has arrived in rather a state of excitement. She insists upon seeing me. She is waiting now in the sitting room.

"Now when young ladies wander about the city at this hour and wake up sleepy people, I presume they have something very urgent to communicate. Should it prove to be an interesting case, I am sure you would wish to follow it from the beginning. At any rate, I thought that I should call you and give you the chance.''

"My dear fellow, I would not miss it for anything."

I had no keener pleasure than in following Holmes in his investigations and in admiring his rapid **deductions**. These deductions were as swift as intuitions. Yet they were always based on logic.

I rapidly threw on my clothes. In a few minutes I was ready to accompany my friend down to the sitting room. A lady dressed in black and heavily veiled sat by the window. She rose as we entered.

"Good morning, madam," said Holmes, cheerily. "My name is Sherlock Holmes. This is my close friend and associate, Dr. Watson. You may speak as freely in front of him as you do to me.

"Ha! I am glad to see that Mrs. Hudson has had the good sense to light the fire. Please draw nearer to it, and I shall order you a cup of hot coffee. I observe that you are shivering.''

"It is not cold which makes me shiver," said the woman in a low voice. However, she changed her seat as requested.

"What, then?"

"It is fear, Mr. Holmes. It is terror."

She raised her veil as she spoke. We could see that she was indeed in a pitiable state of **agitation**. Her face was careworn and gray. And she had restless, frightened eyes, like those of some hunted animal.

Her features and figure were those of a woman of thirty. But her hair was sprinkled with gray, and her expression was weary and worn. Sherlock Holmes glanced at her with one of his quick, all-**comprehensive** glances.

"You must not fear," said he soothingly. He bent forward and patted her forearm. "We shall soon set matters right, I have no doubt. You have come in by train this morning, I see."

"You know me, then?"

"No, but I observe half of a return ticket in the palm of your left glove. You must have started early. Yet you had a good drive in a cart along rough roads before you reached the station."

The lady gave a violent jump. She stared in bewilderment at my companion.

"There is no mystery, my dear madam," said he smiling. "The left arm of your jacket is spattered with mud in no less than seven places. The marks are perfectly fresh. There is no vehicle but a cart which tosses up mud in that way. And then it only does so when you sit on the left-hand side of the driver."

"Whatever your reasons may be, you are perfectly correct," said she. "I started from home before six. I reached Leatherhead at twenty past and came in by the first train to Waterloo.

"Sir, I can stand this strain no longer. I shall go mad if it continues. I have no one to turn to—none, except one, who cares for me. And he, poor fellow, can be of little aid.

"I have heard of you, Mr. Holmes. I have heard of you from Mrs. Farintosh, whom you helped in the hour of her great need. It was from her that I had your address.

"Oh, sir, don't you think that you could help me, too? Perhaps you could throw at least a little light through the dense darkness which surrounds me.

"At present, I cannot reward you for your services. But in a month or six weeks I shall be married and have control of my own income. Then you shall find that I will gratefully pay you."

Holmes turned to his desk. Unlocking it, he drew out a small casebook, which he checked.

"Farintosh," said he. "Ah yes, I recall the case. It concerned an opal crown. I think it was before your time, Watson.

"I can only say, madam, that I shall be happy to give your case the same care as I gave that of your friend. As to reward, my profession is its own reward. But you are free to pay my expenses at the time which suits you best.

"And now I beg that you tell everything that may help us in forming an opinion upon the matter."

"Alas!" replied our visitor, "the very horror of my situation lies in the fact that my fears are so vague. My suspicions depend so entirely upon small points. They might seem trivial to another.

"In fact, even my husband-to-be thinks that what I tell him about it is the fancy of a nervous woman. He does not say so. Yet I can read it from his soothing answers and the way he turns away his eyes.

"But I have heard, Mr. Holmes, that you can see deeply into the many wickednesses of the human heart. You may be able to advise me how to walk amid the dangers which surround me."

"I am all attention, madam."

"My name is Helen Stoner, and I am living with my step-father. He is the last survivor of one of the oldest Saxon[1] families in England, the Roylotts. The family lives at Stoke Moran, on the western border of Surrey."

Holmes nodded his head. "The name is familiar to me," said he.

"The family was at one time among the richest in England. Their land extended over the borders into Berkshire in the north and Hampshire in the west.

"But in the last century, four heirs—one after another—were immoral and wasteful. The family was finally completely ruined by a gambler during the early 1800s. Nothing was left except a few acres of ground and the two-hundred-year-old house, which is itself under a heavy mortgage. The

---

[1]The Saxons were a tribe with German roots. They conquered and settled in Britain during the fifth and sixth centuries.

last owner dragged out his existence there, living the horrible life of an **aristocratic** beggar.

"But his only son, my stepfather, saw that he must adapt himself to the new conditions. So he borrowed some money from a relative. This enabled him to take a medical degree.

"After that, he went to Calcutta.[2] There, by his skill and his force of character, he set up a large practice.

"However, some robberies in his house led to his downfall. In a fit of anger, he blamed his Indian butler and beat him to death.

"My stepfather narrowly escaped a death sentence. As it was, he suffered a long term of imprisonment. Afterwards he returned to England a bitter and disappointed man.

"When Dr. Roylott was in India, he married my mother, Mrs. Stoner. She was the young widow of Major General Stoner, of the Bengal Artillery.[3]

"My sister Julia and I were twins. We were only two years old at the time of my mother's remarriage. She had a large sum of money—not less than 1000 pounds[4] a year. She willed all this to Dr. Roylott while we lived with him. She stated, however, that a certain annual sum should be given to Julia and I in case we should marry.

"Shortly after our return to England my mother died. She was killed eight years ago in a railway accident near Crewe.

"Dr. Roylott then abandoned his attempts to set up a practice in London. Instead, he took us to live with him in the old home of his ancestors at Stoke Moran. The money which my mother had left was enough for all our wants. There seemed to be nothing to stand in the way of our happiness.

"But a terrible change came over our stepfather about this time. One might have thought he would attempt to make friends and visit our neighbors, who had at first been over-

[2]Calcutta is a large city in India. Britain ruled India from 1858-1947.

[3]The Bengal Artillery was a British army unit stationed in India.

[4]The pound is a British sum of money. At the time of the story, a pound was worth about five dollars.

joyed to see a Roylott return. But, instead, he shut himself up in his house. He seldom came out except to start a ferocious quarrel with whoever might cross his path.

"Violence of temper that borders on madness is a trait in the men of the family. In my stepfather's case, I believe it had been made worse by his long stay in the tropics.

"A series of disgraceful fights took place. Two ended in the police court. At last my stepfather became the terror of the village. Folks would fly at his approach, for he is a man of great strength and absolutely uncontrollable temper.

"Last week he hurled the local blacksmith over a wall into a stream. It was only by paying all the money I could gather that I was able to prevent another scandal.

"My stepfather has no friends at all apart from the wandering gypsies. He gives them permission to camp on the few acres of thorny land that are left of the family estate. In return, he accepts the hospitality of their tents. Sometimes he wanders away with them for weeks on end.

"He also has a passion for Indian animals. They are sent over to him by someone he writes to. At this moment, he has a cheetah and a baboon. The two wander freely over his grounds. They are feared by the villagers almost as much as their master.

"You can imagine from what I say that my poor sister Julia and I had no great pleasure in our lives. No servant would stay with us. For a long time we did all the housework.

"Julia was just thirty at the time of her death. Yet her hair had already begun to whiten, even as mine has."

"Your sister is dead, then?"

"She died just two years ago. It is about her death that I wish to speak to you. You can understand that, living as I described, we were not likely to see anyone of our own age and position.

"However, we had an aunt. She was my mother's maiden

sister, Miss Honoria Westphail. She lives near Harrow. We were sometimes allowed to pay short visits to this lady's house.

"Julia went there at Christmas two years ago. There she met a retired major of marines to whom she became engaged.

"My stepfather learned of the engagement when my sister returned. He offered no objection to the marriage. But two weeks before the wedding day, the terrible event occurred which **deprived** me of my only companion."

Sherlock Holmes had been leaning back in his chair with his eyes closed and his head sunk in a cushion. But he half opened his lids now and glanced across at his visitor.

"Please be precise about all details," he said.

"It is easy for me to be so. Every event of that dreadful time is burned into my memory. The manor house is, as I have already said, very old. Only one wing is now used. The bedrooms in this wing are on the ground floor. The sitting rooms are in the central block of the buildings.

"Of these bedrooms the first is Dr. Roylott's, the second my sister's, and the third my own. There is no way to pass directly from one bedroom to another. However, they all open out onto the same corridor. Do I make myself plain?"

"Perfectly so."

"The windows of the three rooms open out upon the lawn. That fatal night Dr. Roylott had gone to his room early. We knew, however, that he had not gone to his bedroom to rest. My sister was bothered by the smell of the strong Indian cigars which he often smoked.

"Therefore, she left her room and came into mine. She sat there for some time, chatting about her upcoming wedding.

"At eleven o'clock she rose to leave me. But she paused at the door and looked back.

" 'Tell me, Helen,' said she, 'have you ever heard

anyone whistle in the dead of the night?'

" 'Never,' said I.

" 'I suppose that you could not possibly whistle, yourself, in your sleep?'

" 'Certainly not. But why?'

" 'Because during the last few nights I have heard a low, clear whistle. I hear it at about three in the morning. I am a light sleeper, and it came from—perhaps from the next room, perhaps from the lawn. I thought that I would just ask you if you had heard it.'

" 'No, I have not. It must be those wretched gypsies.'

" 'Very likely. Yet if it were on the lawn, I wonder why you did not hear it also?'

" 'Ah, but I sleep more heavily than you.'

" 'Well, it is of no great importance, at any rate.' She smiled back at me and closed my door. A few moments later I heard her key turn in the lock.''

"Indeed," said Holmes. "Was it your custom always to lock yourselves in at night?"

"Always."

"And why?"

"I think that I mentioned to you that the doctor kept a cheetah and a baboon. We did not feel secure unless our doors were locked."

"Quite so. Please go on with your statement."

"I could not sleep that night. I had a vague feeling of **impending** misfortune. As I told you, my sister and I were twins. You know how mysterious the links are which bind two such close souls.

"It was a wild night. The wind was howling outside, and the rain was beating and splashing against the windows.

"Suddenly, amid all the racket of the storm, the wild scream of a terrified woman burst out. I knew that it was my sister's voice.

"I sprang from my bed, wrapped a shawl round me, and

rushed into the hall. As I opened my door I seemed to hear a low whistle. It was like the sound my sister had described. A few moments later I heard a clanging sound, as if a heavy metal object had fallen.

"As I ran down the passage, my sister's door was unlocked and swung slowly on its hinges. I stared at it horror-stricken, not knowing what was about to come out.

"By the light of the lamp in the hall I saw my sister appear at the door. Her face was pale with terror and her hands were stretched out for help. Her whole figure swayed to and fro like that of a drunkard.

"I ran to her and threw my arms round her. But at that moment her knees seemed to give way and she fell to the ground. She **writhed** like one who is in terrible pain and her limbs were dreadfully twisted.

"At first I thought that she had not recognized me. But as I bent over her, she suddenly shrieked out in a voice which I shall never forget.

" 'Oh, my God! Helen! It was the band! The speckled band!'

"There was something else which she wanted to say. She stabbed with her finger into the air in the direction of the doctor's room. But a fresh fit seized her and choked her words.

"I rushed out, calling loudly for my stepfather. I met him hurrying from his room in his robe.

"When he reached my sister's side, she was unconscious. Though he poured brandy down her throat and sent for medical aid, all efforts were in vain. She slowly faded and died without having recovered consciousness. That was the dreadful end of my beloved sister."

"One moment," said Holmes. "Are you sure about this whistle and metallic sound? Could you swear to it?"

"That was what the county coroner asked me at the inquest.[5] It is my strong impression that I heard it. Yet with

[5]A coroner is an official who decides the cause of death when a case involves violence or suspicious circumstances. An inquest is the public hearing where evidence about a death is presented.

the crashing of the storm and the creaking of an old house, I may have been deceived.''

"Was your sister dressed?''

"No, she was in her nightgown. In her right hand was found the burned stump of a match. In her left was a matchbox.''

"Showing that she struck a light and looked about when the alarm took place. That is important. And what conclusions did the coroner come to?''

"He investigated the case with great care. You see, Dr. Roylott's behavior had long been gossiped about in the county.

"But the coroner was unable to find any good explanation for her death. My evidence showed that the door had been locked on the inside. The windows were blocked by old-fashioned shutters with broad iron bars. Those shutters were closed every night.

"The walls were carefully examined. They were proven to be quite solid all the way round the room. The flooring was also thoroughly examined, with the same result. The chimney is wide but is barred up by four large staples.

"It is certain, therefore, that my sister was quite alone when she met her end. Besides, there were no marks of any violence on her.''

"What about poison?''

"The doctors examined her for it, but could not find any traces.''

"What do you think that this unfortunate lady died of, then?''

"It is my belief that she died of pure fear and nervous shock. But what it was that frightened her, I cannot imagine.''

"Were there gypsies on the estate at the time?''

"Yes, there are nearly always some there.''

"Ah, and what did you gather from this reference to a

band—a speckled band?''

"Sometimes I have thought that it was merely the wild talk of delirium. Sometimes I considered that it may have referred to a band of people—perhaps to the gypsies. I do not know if the spotted handkerchiefs which so many of them wear might have led her to use that strange phrase."

Holmes shook his head like a man who is far from being satisfied.

"These are very deep waters," said he. "Please go on with your story."

"Two years have passed since then. Until lately my life had been lonelier than ever.

"However, a month ago, a dear friend whom I have known for many years asked me to marry him. His name is Armitage—Percy Armitage. He is the second son of Mr. Armitage of Crane Walter, near Reading. My stepfather has not objected to the match, and we are to be married in the spring.

"Two days ago some repairs were started in the west wing of the building. A hole was made in one of my bedroom walls. Therefore, I have had to move into the room where my sister died and sleep in the very bed where she slept.

"Imagine, then, the terror I felt last night when it began to happen again. I was lying awake, thinking over her terrible fate. Suddenly I heard in the silence of the night the low whistle which had come just before her own death.

"I sprang up and lit the lamp. But nothing was to be seen in the room. I was too shaken to go to bed again, however, so I dressed.

"As soon as it was daylight, I slipped down, got a cart at the nearby Crown Inn, and drove to Leatherhead. From there I have come on the morning train with the one object of seeing you and asking your advice."

"You have done wisely," said my friend. "But have you told me all?"

"Yes, all."

"Miss Roylott, you have not. You are screening your stepfather."

"Why, what do you mean?"

For answer Holmes pushed back the frill of black lace which fringed the visitor's hand. Five little black and blue spots—the marks of four fingers and a thumb—were printed upon the white wrist.

"You have been cruelly abused," said Holmes.

The lady blushed deeply and covered her injured wrist. "He is a rough man," said she. "Perhaps he hardly knows his own strength."

There was a long silence. Holmes leaned his chin upon his hands and stared into the crackling fire.

"This is a very deep business," he said at last. "There are a thousand details I would like to know before I decide upon our course of action. Yet we have not a moment to lose.

"If we were to come to Stoke Moran today, could we see these rooms without the knowledge of your stepfather?"

"As it happens, he spoke of coming into town today on some most important business. He will probably be away all day. There would be nothing to disturb you. We have a housekeeper now, but she is old and foolish. I could easily get her out of the way."

"Excellent. You are not **averse** to this trip, Watson?"

"By no means."

"Then we shall both come. What are you going to do yourself?"

"I have one or two things I wish to do now that I am in town. But I shall return by the twelve o'clock train to be there in time for your arrival."

"And you may expect us early in the afternoon. I myself have some small business matters to attend to. Will you not stay and eat breakfast with us?"

"No, I must go. My heart is lightened already since I have told my trouble to you. I shall look forward to seeing you again this afternoon."

She dropped her thick black veil over her face and glided from the room.

"And what do you think of it all, Watson?" asked Sherlock Holmes, leaning back in his chair.

"It seems to me to be a most dark and sinister business."

"Dark enough and sinister enough."

"Yet what if the lady is correct that the floor and walls are solid and the door, window, and chimney are blocked? Then her sister must have been alone when she met her mysterious end."

"What of these whistles at night and the very peculiar words of the dying woman?"

"I cannot imagine."

"But let's combine the ideas. First, think of the whistles at night. Second, consider the gypsies who are on close terms with this old doctor. Third is the fact that we have every reason to believe the doctor has an interest in preventing his stepdaughter's marriage. Fourth is the girl's dying reference to a band.

"Finally, add the fact that Miss Helen Stoner heard a metallic clang. This might have been caused by one of those metal bars which secured the shutters falling back into their place.

"I think there is good reason to believe that the mystery may be cleared up if we combine those facts."

"But what, then, did the gypsies do?"

"I cannot imagine."

"I see many objections to any such theory."

"And so do I. It is precisely for that reason that we are going to Stoke Moran today. I want to see if the objections will destroy my case, or if they may be explained away. But what in the name of the devil!"

My companion's exclamation was due to the fact that our door had been suddenly dashed open. A huge man stood there in the doorway.

His costume was a peculiar mix of the professional and of the agricultural. He wore a black top hat, a long coat, and a pair of high gaiters.[6] In his hand he swung a hunting stick.

He was so tall that his hat actually brushed the top of the doorway. His width seemed to span it across from side to side. His large face was crossed with a thousand wrinkles and burned yellow by the sun. It was marked with every evil passion. He turned from one to the other of us.

He had deep-set, red eyes and a high, thin, fleshless nose. Together, they made him somewhat resemble a fierce old bird of prey.

"Which of you is Holmes?" asked this weird figure.

"That is my name, sir. But you have the advantage of me," said my companion, quietly.

"I am Dr. Grimesby Roylott of Stoke Moran."

"Indeed, doctor," said Holmes **blandly**. "Please sit down."

"I will do nothing of the kind. My stepdaughter has been here. I have traced her. What has she been saying to you?"

"It is a little cold for this time of the year," said Holmes.

"What has she been saying to you?" screamed the old man furiously.

"But I have heard that the spring flowers should be lovely," continued my companion coolly.

"Ha! You put me off, do you?" said our new visitor. He took a step forward and shook his hunting stick. "I know you, you scoundrel! I have heard of you before. You are Holmes, the meddler."

My friend smiled.

"Holmes, the busybody!"

His smile broadened.

---

[6]Gaiters are leather or cloth coverings for the lower leg.

"Holmes, the Scotland Yard Jack-in-office!"[7]

Holmes chuckled heartily. "Your conversation is most entertaining," said he. "When you go out, close the door. There is definitely a draft."

"I will go when I have said my say. Don't you dare to meddle with my affairs. I know that Miss Stoner has been here. I traced her! I am a dangerous man to cross! See here."

He stepped swiftly forward and seized the poker. With his huge brown hands, he bent it into a curve.

"See that you keep yourself out of my grip," he snarled. Then hurling the twisted poker into the fireplace, he strode out of the room.

"He seems a very friendly person," said Holmes laughing. "I am not quite so bulky. Yet if he had remained, I might have shown him that my grip is not much more feeble than his own."

As he spoke he picked up the steel poker. With a sudden effort, he straightened it out again.

"Imagine his having the nerve to confuse me with the official detective force! However, this incident gives zest to our investigation. I only trust that our little friend will not suffer from her carelessness in allowing this brute to trace her.

"And now, Watson, we shall order breakfast. Afterwards I shall walk down to Doctors' Commons.[8] There I hope to get some data which may help us in this matter."

It was nearly one o'clock when Sherlock Holmes returned from his trip. He held in his hand a sheet of blue paper, scrawled with notes and figures.

"I have seen the will of the dead wife," said he. "To determine its exact meaning I have had to work out the present prices of the investments involved.

"At the time of the wife's death, the total income was

[7]Scotland Yard is the cite of London police headquarters. Jack-in-offices are minor officials who are vain about their position.

[8]The offices of civil lawyers (as opposed to criminal lawyers) are located in the Doctors' Commons.

just short of 1100 pounds. Now, because agricultural prices have fallen, it is not more than 750 pounds. If they married, each daughter could claim an income of 250 pounds.

"Therefore, it is clear that if both girls had married, the good doctor would have been left with a mere **pittance**. Even the marriage of one would reduce his income to a very serious extent.

"Well, my morning's work has not been wasted. I have proved that he has the very strongest motives for standing in the way of any marriage.

"And now, Watson, this is too serious for **dawdling**. It is even more serious since the old man is aware that we are interesting ourselves in his affairs.

"So if you are ready, we shall call a cab and drive to Waterloo Station. I should be very much obliged if you would slip your revolver into your pocket. A gun is an excellent argument with gentlemen who can twist steel pokers into knots. That and a toothbrush are all that we need, I think."

At Waterloo we were fortunate in catching a train for Leatherhead. There we hired a cart at an inn and drove for four or five miles through the lovely Surrey lanes.

It was a perfect day, with a bright sun and a few fleecy clouds in the heavens. The trees and roadside hedges were just shooting out their first green buds. The air was full of the pleasant smell of the moist earth. To me at least there was a strange contrast between the sweet promise of the spring and this sinister quest we were on.

My companion sat in the front of the cart. His arms were folded, his hat pulled down over his eyes, and his chin sunk upon his breast. He was buried in the deepest thought.

Suddenly, however, he quickly stirred. Tapping me on the shoulder, he pointed over the meadows.

"Look there!" said he.

A heavily wooded park stretched up a gentle slope. At

the top of the hill, it became a grove. From amid the branches there jutted the gray peaks and high roof of a very old mansion.

"Stoke Moran?" said he.

"Yes, sir, that be the house of Dr. Grimesby Roylott," remarked the driver.

"There is some building going on there," said Holmes. "That is where we are going."

"There's the village," said the driver. He pointed to a cluster of roofs some distance to the left. "But if you want to get to the house, you'll find it shorter to get over this stile.[9] Then take the footpath over the fields. There it is, where the lady is walking."

"And the lady, I imagine, is Miss Stoner," observed Holmes, shading his eyes. "Yes, I think we had better do as you suggest."

We got off, paid our fare, and the cart rattled back on its way to Leatherhead.

"I thought it best," said Holmes as we climbed the stile, "that this fellow should think we had come here as architects or on some business. It may stop his gossip.

"Good afternoon, Miss Stoner. You see that we have been as good as our word."

Our client of the morning had hurried forward to meet us with a face which spoke her joy.

"I have been waiting so eagerly for you," she cried, shaking hands with us warmly. "All has turned out splendidly. Dr. Roylott has gone to town. It is unlikely that he will be back before evening."

"We have had the pleasure of being introduced to the doctor," said Holmes. In a few words he sketched out what had occurred. Miss Stoner turned white to the lips as she listened.

"Good heavens!" she cried. "He has followed me, then."

"So it appears."

---

[9]A stile is a short staircase for getting over a fence.

"He is so cunning that I never know when I am safe from him. What will he say when he returns?"

"He must guard himself. He may find that there is someone more cunning than himself upon his track.

"You must lock yourself up from him tonight. If he is violent, we shall take you away to your aunt's at Harrow. Now, we must make the best use of our time. So kindly take us at once to the rooms which we are to examine."

The building was of gray stone, covered with blotches of lichen.[10] It had a high central portion and two curving wings. These wings, thrown out on each side, looked like the claws of a crab.

In one of these wings the windows were broken and blocked with wooden boards. The roof over this wing was partly caved in. It was the picture of ruin. The central portion was in little better repair.

In comparison, the right-hand wing looked modern. The blinds in the windows and the blue smoke curling up from the chimneys showed that the family resided here.

A wooden framework had been built against the end wall and the stonework had been broken into. But there were no signs of any workmen at the moment of our visit.

Holmes walked slowly up and down the poorly trimmed lawn. He examined with deep attention the outsides of the windows.

"This window, I take it, belongs to the room in which you used to sleep? The center one is your sister's? And the one next to the main building is Dr. Roylott's chamber?"

"Exactly so. But I am now sleeping in the middle one."

"Until the repairs are made, as I understand. By the way, there does not seem to be any very urgent need for repairs at that end wall."

"There were none. I believe that it was an excuse to move me from my room."

"Ah! That is significant. Now, on the other side of this

---

[10]Lichen is a scaly, dry-looking plant of yellow or gray color. It grows on rocks, tree trunks, and walls.

narrow wing runs the hallway that is off of these three rooms. There are windows in it, of course?''

''Yes, but very small ones. Too narrow for anyone to climb through.''

''Since you both locked your doors at night, your rooms could not be entered from that side. Now, would you have the kindness to go into your room and bar your shutters.''

Miss Stoner did so. After a careful examination, Holmes tried in every way to force the shutter open. But he had no success. There was no slit through which a knife could be passed to raise the bar.

Then with his magnifying lens he tested the hinges. They proved to be of solid iron, built firmly into the thick stonework.

''Hum!'' said he, scratching his chin in some **perplexity**. ''My theory is certainly running into some difficulties. No one could open these shutters if they were bolted. Well, we shall see if the inside throws any light upon the matter.''

A small side door led into the whitewashed hallway off the three bedrooms. Holmes refused to examine the third room. Therefore, we passed at once to the second. This was the room in which Miss Stoner was now sleeping and in which her sister had met her fate.

It was a simple little room, with a low ceiling and a **gaping** fireplace, in the style of old country houses. A brown chest of drawers stood in one corner. A narrow bed with a white spread stood in another. A dressing table was placed on the left-hand side of the window.

These articles, with two small wicker chairs, were the only furniture in the room except for a square of carpet in the center. The boards and wall paneling were of brown, worm-eaten oak. The wood was old and discolored. It looked like it may have dated from the original building of the house.

Holmes drew one of the chairs into a corner and sat silent. His eyes traveled round and round and up and down, taking in every detail of the apartment.

"Where does that bell communicate with?" he asked, at last. He pointed to a thick bell rope[11] which hung down beside the bed. The tassel actually laid on the pillow.

"It goes to the housekeeper's room."

"It looks newer than the other things."

"Yes, it was only put there a couple of years ago."

"Your sister asked for it, I suppose?"

"No, I never heard of her using it. We used always to get what we wanted for ourselves."

"Indeed, it seemed unnecessary to put so nice a bell rope there. You will excuse me for a few minutes while I satisfy myself about this floor."

He threw himself down upon his face with his lens in his hand. Crawling swiftly backward and forward, he closely examined the cracks between the boards. Then he did the same with the wood paneling.

At last he walked over to the bed. He spent some time in staring at it. He ran his eye up and down the wall as well. Finally he took the bell rope in his hand and gave it a brisk tug.

"Why, it's a dummy," said he.

"Won't it ring?"

"No, it is not even attached to a wire. This is very interesting. You can see now that it is fastened to a hook just above the little opening for the ventilator."[12]

"How very absurd! I never noticed that before."

"Very strange!" muttered Holmes, pulling at the rope. "There are one or two very odd points about this room. For example, what a fool a builder must have been to put a ventilator between two rooms. With the same trouble, he might have placed it on the outer wall so that it brought in air from the outside!"

"That is also quite modern," said the lady.

[11]A bell rope was a device used to call servants. When the rope was pulled, it rang a bell in a servant's room.

[12]A ventilator is a small opening that admits fresh air into a room.

"Done about the same time as the bell rope?" remarked Holmes.

"Yes, there were several little changes carried out about that time."

"They seem to have been of a most interesting character: bell ropes which do not work and ventilators which do not ventilate. With your permission, Miss Stoner, we shall now carry our researches into the last room."

Dr. Grimesby Roylott's room was larger than that of his stepdaughter. But it was as plainly furnished. A cot, a small wooden shelf full of books (mostly technical works), an armchair beside the bed, a plain wooden chair against the wall, a round table, and a large iron safe were the main things which met the eye. Holmes walked slowly round. He examined each and all of these things with the keenest interest.

"What's in here?" he asked, tapping the safe.

"My stepfather's business papers."

"Oh! You have seen inside, then?"

"Only once, some years ago. I remember that it was full of papers."

"There isn't a cat in it, for example?"

"No. What a strange idea!"

"Well, look at this!" He took up a small saucer of milk which stood on the top of it.

"No, we don't keep a cat. But there are a cheetah and a baboon."

"Ah, yes, of course! Well, a cheetah is just a big cat. Yet a saucer of milk does not go very far in satisfying its wants, I dare say. There is one point which I should wish to determine."

He squatted down in front of the wooden chair. He examined the seat of it with the greatest attention.

"Thank you. That is quite settled," said he. He rose and put his lens in his pocket.

"Hello! Here is something interesting!"

The object which had caught his eye was a small dog leash hung on one corner of the bed. The leash, however, was curled upon itself and tied so as to make a loop.

"What do you make of that, Watson?"

"It's a common enough leash. But I don't know why it should be tied."

"That is not quite so common, is it? Ah, me! It's a wicked world. When a clever man turns his brains to crime it is the worst of all.

"I think that I have seen enough now, Miss Stoner. With your permission, we shall walk out upon the lawn."

I had never seen my friend's face so grim or his brow so dark as when we left the scene of this investigation. Neither Miss Stoner nor myself liked to break in upon his thoughts. So we had walked several times up and down the lawn before he spoke.

"It is very essential, Miss Stoner," said he, "that you should follow my advice in every detail."

"I shall most certainly do so."

"The matter is too serious for any hesitation. Your life may depend upon your **compliance**."

"I assure you that I am in your hands."

"In the first place, both my friend and I must spend the night in your room."

Both Miss Stoner and I gazed at him in astonishment.

"Yes, it must be so. Let me explain. I believe that is the village inn over there?"

"Yes, that is the Crown."

"Very good. Your windows would be visible from there?"

"Certainly."

"You must shut yourself in your room when your step-father comes back. Use the **pretense** that you have a headache. Then, when you hear him go to bed for the night, you must open the shutters of your window. Put your lamp there as a signal to us.

"Then leave quietly with everything you are likely to want. Go to the room where you used to sleep. I have no doubt that, in spite of the repairs, you could manage there for one night."

"Oh yes, easily."

"The rest you will leave in our hands."

"But what will you do?"

"We shall spend the night in your room. And we shall investigate the cause of this noise which has disturbed you."

"I believe, Mr. Holmes, that you have already made up your mind," said Miss Stoner. She laid her hand upon my companion's sleeve.

"Perhaps I have."

"Then for pity's sake, tell me what caused my sister's death."

"I should prefer to have clearer proofs before I speak."

"You can at least tell me whether my own thought is correct. Did she die from some sudden fright?"

"No, I do not think so. I think that there was probably some more direct cause. And now, Miss Stoner, we must leave you. If Dr. Roylott returned and saw us, our journey would be in vain.

"Goodbye, and be brave," Holmes continued. "If you will do what I have told you, you may rest assured that we shall soon drive away the dangers that threaten you."

Sherlock Holmes and I had no difficulty in getting a bedroom and sitting room at the Crown Inn. The rooms were on the upper floor. From our window we had a view of the gate and the right-hand wing of Stoke Moran.

At dusk we saw Dr. Grimesby Roylott drive past. His huge form loomed up beside the little figure of the lad who drove him. The boy had some slight difficulty in undoing the heavy iron gates. We heard the hoarse roar of the doctor's voice. And we saw the fury with which he shook his clenched fists at the boy.

The cart drove on. A few minutes later we saw a sudden light spring up among the trees. A lamp had been lit in one of the sitting rooms.

"I think you should know something, Watson," said Holmes, as we sat together in the gathering darkness. "I really have some **scruples** about taking you with me tonight. There is a definite element of danger."

"Can I be of assistance?"

"Your presence might be invaluable."

"Then I shall certainly come."

"It is very kind of you."

"You speak of danger. You have evidently seen more in these rooms than was visible to me."

"No, but I fancy that I may have deduced a little more. I imagine that you saw all that I did."

"I saw nothing unusual except the bell rope. What purpose that serves is more than I can imagine, I must confess."

"You saw the ventilator, too?"

"Yes, but I do not think it is so unusual to have a small opening between two rooms. It was so small that a rat could hardly pass through."

"I knew that we should find a ventilator before we ever came to Stoke Moran."

"My dear Holmes!"

"Oh yes, I did. You remember in her statement she said that her sister could smell Dr. Roylott's cigar. Now, of course, that suggested at once that there must be an opening between the two rooms. It could only have been a small one or it would have been mentioned at the coroner's inquest. I deduced a ventilator."

"But what harm can there be in that?"

"Well, the order in which things happened is at least a curious coincidence. A ventilator is made, a cord is hung, and a lady who sleeps in the bed dies. Doesn't that strike you as being strange?''

"I cannot as yet see any connection."

"Did you observe anything very peculiar about that bed?"

"No."

"It was clamped to the floor. Did you ever see a bed fastened like that before?''

"I cannot say that I have."

"The lady could not move her bed. It was always supposed to be in the same position to the ventilator and to the rope. I call it a rope, for it was clearly never meant for a bell rope.''

"Holmes," I cried, "I seem to see dimly what you are hinting at. We are only just in time to prevent some mysterious and horrible crime.''

"Mysterious enough and horrible enough. When a doctor does go wrong, he is the worst of criminals. He has nerve and he has knowledge. Palmer and Pritchard were among the heads of their profession.

"This man strikes even deeper. But I think, Watson, that we shall be able to strike deeper still.

"But we shall have horrors enough before the night is over. For goodness' sake, let us quietly smoke our pipes. We shall turn our minds for a few hours to something more cheerful.''

About nine o'clock the light among the trees was **extinguished**. All was dark in the direction of the manor house. Two hours passed slowly away. Then, suddenly, just at the stroke of eleven, a single bright light shone out right in front of us.

"That is our signal," said Holmes, springing to his feet. "It comes from the middle window."

As we went out, Holmes said a few words to the landlord. He explained that we were going on a late visit to a friend. He added that we might spend the night there.

A moment later we were out on the dark road. A chill

wind blew in our faces. One yellow light twinkled in front of us through the gloom to guide us on our somber errand.

We had little trouble in entering the grounds. Unrepaired holes gaped in the old park wall. Making our way among the trees, we reached the lawn and crossed it.

We were about to enter through the window, when out from some laurel bushes there darted what seemed to be a hideous and distorted child. This creature threw itself upon the grass with writhing limbs. Then it ran swiftly across the lawn into the darkness.

"My God!" I whispered. "Did you see it?"

Holmes was for the moment as startled as I. His hand closed like a clamp upon my wrist in his agitation. Then he broke into a low laugh and put his lips to my ear.

"It is a nice household," he murmured. "That is the baboon."

I had forgotten the strange pets which the doctor kept. There was a cheetah, too. Perhaps we might find it upon our shoulders at any moment.

I confess that I felt better when, following Holmes' example and slipping off my shoes, I found myself inside the bedroom. My companion noiselessly closed the shutters. After that he moved the lamp onto the table and cast his eyes round the room.

All was as we had seen it in the daytime. Creeping up to me, Holmes made a trumpet of his hand. Then he gently whispered into my ear again. He spoke so softly that I could barely make out the words.

"The least sound would be fatal to our plans."

I nodded to show that I had heard.

"We must sit without light. He would see it through the ventilator."

I nodded again.

"Do not go to sleep. Your very life may depend upon it. Have your pistol ready in case we should need it. I will sit on the side of the bed. You take that chair."

I took out my revolver and laid it on the corner of the table.

Holmes had brought a long thin cane. This he placed upon the bed beside him. By it he laid the box of matches and the stump of a candle. Then he turned down the lamp, and we were left in darkness.

How shall I ever forget that dreadful **vigil**? I could not hear a sound, not even the drawing of a breath. Yet I knew that my companion sat open-eyed, within a few feet of me, as nervous and tense as I was.

The shutters cut off the least ray of light. So we waited in absolute darkness. From outside came the occasional cry of a night bird.

Once at our very window we heard a long, drawn-out, catlike whine. The call told us that the cheetah was indeed on the loose.

Far away we could hear the deep tones of the church clock, which boomed out every quarter of an hour. How long they seemed, those quarters! Twelve struck and one and two and three. Still we sat waiting silently for whatever might happen.

Suddenly there was the momentary gleam of a light up in the direction of the ventilator. This vanished immediately. But it was followed by a strong smell of burning oil and heated metal. Someone in the next room had lit a dark lantern.

I heard a gentle sound of movement. Then all was silent once more, though the smell grew stronger. For half an hour I sat with straining ears.

Then suddenly I heard another sound. It was a very gentle, soothing sound, like that of a small jet of steam escaping from a kettle.

The instant we heard it, Holmes sprang from the bed.

He struck a match and lashed furiously with his cane at the bell pull.

"You see it, Watson?" he yelled. "You see it?"

But I saw nothing. At the moment when Holmes lit the match, I heard a low, clear whistle. But the sudden glare flashing in my weary eyes made it impossible for me to tell what my friend lashed at so savagely. I could, however, see that his face was deadly pale and filled with horror and hatred.

Holmes finally ceased striking. Then, as he gazed up at the ventilator, there suddenly broke from the silence the most horrible cry I have ever heard. It swelled up louder and louder. It was a hoarse yell of pain, fear, and anger all mingled in one dreadful shriek.

They say that way down in the village and even in the distant parson's house that cry raised sleepers from their beds. It struck cold to our hearts. I stood gazing at Holmes and he at me until the last echoes had died away into silence.

"What can it mean?" I gasped.

"It means that it is all over," Holmes answered. "And perhaps, after all, it is for the best. Take your pistol. We will enter Dr. Roylott's room."

With a grave face he lit the lamp and led the way down the hall. Twice he knocked at the door without any reply from within. Then he turned the handle and entered. I followed on his heels, with the pistol ready in my hand.

It was a strange sight which met our eyes. On the table stood a dark lantern with the shutter half open. It threw a brilliant beam of light upon the iron safe, the door of which was open.

Beside this table, on the wooden chair, sat Dr. Grimesby Roylott. He was dressed in a long gray robe. His bare ankles were **protruding** from beneath. His feet were thrust into red, heelless Turkish slippers.

Across his lap lay the short cane with the long lash which

we had noticed during the day. His chin was cocked upward. His eyes were fixed in a dreadful, rigid stare at the corner of the ceiling.

Round his forehead he had a peculiar yellow band with brownish speckles. This band seemed to be bound tightly round his head. As we entered he made neither sound nor motion.

"The band! The speckled band!" whispered Holmes.

I took a step forward. In an instant his strange headgear began to move. From his hair, there reared the squat, diamond-shaped, and puffed neck of a dreadful serpent.

"It is a swamp adder!" cried Holmes. "It is the deadliest snake in India. Roylott must have died within ten seconds of being bitten.

"In truth, violence does backfire on the violent. The schemer falls into the pit which he digs for another.

"Let us thrust this creature back into its den. We can then remove Miss Stoner to some place of shelter and let the police know what has happened."

As he spoke he drew the leash swiftly from the dead man's lap. Throwing the noose round the reptile's neck, he drew it from its horrid perch. Then carrying it at arm's length, he threw it into the iron safe and closed the door.

Such are the true facts of the death of Dr. Grimesby Roylott of Stoke Moran. I need not **prolong** this already long story by telling how we broke the sad news to the terrified girl. And I will not go into details about how we took her by the morning train to her good aunt at Harrow. Nor will I discuss how officials finally concluded that the doctor met his fate while foolishly playing with a dangerous pet.

As we traveled back the next day, Holmes told me the little which I had yet to learn about the case.

"I had," said he, "come to an entirely false conclusion. That shows, my dear Watson, how dangerous it always is to reason from too little data.

"The gypsies and the word 'band,' which the poor girl used (no doubt to explain what she saw by the light of her match) put me upon an entirely wrong scent.

"I can only say for myself that I instantly rethought my views when faced with new evidence. It became clear that whatever danger threatened a person in the room could not come from the window or door.

"My attention was speedily drawn, as I have already said, to this ventilator and bell rope beside the bed. The discovery that the rope was a dummy and that the bed was clamped to the floor gave rise to a new suspicion. I began to see the rope as a bridge for something passing through the hole and coming to the bed.

"The idea of a snake instantly occurred to me. When I tied it with the fact that the doctor was supplied with creatures from India, I felt I was on the right track. Using an untraceable poison was just such an idea that would occur to a clever and ruthless man trained in the East.

"The quick effect of the poison would also, from his point of view, be an advantage. It would be a sharp-eyed coroner, indeed, who would note the two little dark wounds the fangs made.

"Then I thought of the whistle. Of course he must call the snake back before the morning light revealed it to the victim. He had probably trained it to return to him when summoned by using the milk which we saw.

"So, you see, the doctor would put the snake through this ventilator at the hour that he thought best. He was certain that it would crawl down the rope and land on the bed. It might or might not bite the occupant. Perhaps she might escape every night for a week. But sooner or later, she must fall a victim.

"I had come to these conclusions before I had ever entered his room. An inspection of his chair showed me that he had been in the habit of standing on it. Of course this would be necessary in order for him to reach the ventilator.

"The sight of the safe, the milk, and the leash were enough to finally lift any doubts which may have remained. The clang heard by Miss Stoner is easily explained. It was obviously caused by her stepfather hastily closing the door of his safe upon the terrible snake.

"Having once made up my mind, you know the steps which I took to test my theory. I heard the creature hiss, as I have no doubt that you did also. So I instantly lit the light and attacked it."

"With the result of driving it through the ventilator."

"And also with the result of causing it to turn upon its master at the other side. Some of the blows of my cane undoubtedly fell on the snake. Its temper was roused, so it flew upon the first person it saw.

"In this way I am no doubt indirectly responsible for Dr. Grimesby Roylott's death. I cannot say that it is likely to weigh very heavily upon my conscience."

"The Adventure of the Speckled Band" was first published in 1892.

INSIGHTS INTO
ARTHUR CONAN DOYLE

(1859-1930)

After he had been a doctor for a time, Doyle decided to become an eye specialist. He went to Vienna in December 1890 to study.

After four months of study, Doyle returned to London and set up office. During the next five months he practiced as an eye doctor. But he never treated a single patient.

Still, Doyle's decision to become an eye doctor was fortunate. It was this failure that finally pushed him over the brink. In August 1891 he abandoned his medical career and at last became a writer.

Many people know that Doyle wrote the Sherlock Holmes stories. But fewer know that Doyle himself solved several mysteries.

Among his cases, Doyle helped find the stolen Irish Crown Jewels. He helped recover gems stolen during the performance of a Holmes play as well. He also proved a young lawyer innocent of killing cattle. He even cleared a man convicted of murder.

But with one case alone, Doyle showed his detective skills were worthy of Holmes. The case arose when a woman asked Doyle to find her cousin. The man had vanished from a London hotel one night.

Doyle sent her an answer by return mail. He had correctly figured out the man's location—*in less than an hour*.

Doyle greatly influenced the study of crime by his tales. In France, a major crime lab was named after Doyle. In Egypt, the police were trained in Holmes' methods.

Doyle's books were required reading for several police forces in Europe as well. A Scotland Yard official went so far as to say, "It was . . . Doyle who pointed the way to the use of scientific methods in the solution of crime."

Throughout his life, Doyle fought for various causes. Some of the causes he backed were Ireland's right to self-rule, the right to divorce, and the need for reform in the Congo.

One interest consumed the last fifteen years of Doyle's life. One day in 1916, Doyle believed he received a spirit message from his dead brother-in-law. He strongly felt he must show that spirits did exist and could communicate with the world. Doyle spent the rest of his life going to seances and speaking and writing on spiritualism.

The world was shocked when Doyle made his beliefs public. The press ridiculed him. The government decided not to make him a baron because of his strange beliefs.

But Doyle did not waver, either in speaking out or funding his efforts. He may have spent over half a million dollars of his own money to advance the cause.

Doyle always used the same method in writing the Sherlock Holmes stories. He thought of the solution to the crime first. Then he made up the rest of the tale.

Doyle wrote almost constantly, from early morning till late afternoon. He even wrote while standing in line to buy a ticket or waiting for a traffic light to change. When friends visited him, he would keep on writing as they talked. But he never missed a word of the conversation.

One example of his speed is the history of "The Blue Carbuncle" and "The Speckled Band." Doyle wrote both tales in just one week.

continued

Other works by Doyle:
    "Adventure of the Dying Detective," short story
    "Adventure of the Solitary Cyclist," short story
    "The Man with the Twisted Lip," short story
    "The Red-headed League," short story
    The Sign of the Four, novel
    The White Company, novel

THE INTERLOPERS

SAKI

VOCABULARY PREVIEW

Below is a list of words that appear in the story. Read the list and get to know the words before you start the story.

acquiesced—agreed; consented
afforded—provided or offered
affrays—fights; clashes
compact—agreement; bargain
condolences—expressions of sympathy
crest—top; peak
detested—hatcd
fractures—breakages
interlopers—intruders
languor—lack of energy; tiredness
marauders—raiders; bandits
pinioned—tied or pinned
pious—holy; religious
plight—difficult situation
quarry—prey; victim being tracked
reconciliation—renewal of a friendship after a break
  or quarrel
reviving—giving back strength and energy
succor—aid; help
unstrung—having lost one's nerve
wrested—wrenched away

THE INTERLOPERS

SAKI

The feud between the Gradwitzs and Znaeyms is deep and ancient. For years now their hate has simply fed itself.

This night their bloodthirst promises to be quenched at last. Yet when the two foes meet, they find a third enemy with an even greater appetite.

In a forest of mixed trees somewhere in the eastern Carpathians,[1] a man stood one winter night watching and listening. He seemed as though he were waiting for some beast to come within range of his vision, and later, of his rifle.

But the game for which he kept so keen a lookout was not one that was lawfully

[1] The Carpathians mountain range runs through Romania and Czechoslovakia.

and properly on the hunter's list. Ulrich von Gradwitz patrolled the dark forest in quest of a human enemy.

The forests of Gradwitz stretched far and were well stocked with game. The narrow strip of steep woodland on its outskirts was not remarkable for the game that lived there or the shooting it **afforded**. But this strip of land was the most jealously guarded of all its owner's territories.

A famous lawsuit in his grandfather's day had **wrested** it from the illegal possession of a neighboring family. This family of minor landowners had never **acquiesced** in the judgment of the courts. A long series of poaching[2] **affrays** and similar scandals had made relationships between the families bitter for three generations.

The neighbors' feud had grown into a personal one since Ulrich had come to be head of his family. If there was a man in the world whom he **detested** and wished ill to, it was Georg Znaeym. Znaeym was the inheritor of the quarrel and the tireless game snatcher and raider of the land claimed by both sides.

The feud might have died down or been settled if the personal ill will of the two men had not stood in the way. As boys they had thirsted for one another's blood. As men each prayed that misfortune might fall on the other.

This windy winter night Ulrich had banded together his foresters to watch the dark forest. He was not in quest of four-footed **quarry**. He was on the lookout for thieves whom he suspected of prowling from across the boundary.

The deer, which usually stayed under cover during a stormwind, were running like driven things tonight. And there was movement and unrest among the creatures that usually slept through the dark hours. There was indeed a disturbing element in the forest. Ulrich could guess from where it came.

He strayed away by himself from the watchers whom he had placed in ambush on the **crest** of the hill. He wandered

---

[2]Poaching is taking game from another person's land without permission.

far down the steep slopes amid the wild tangle of undergrowth. Peering through the trees and listening through the whistling, shrieking wind and restless beating of branches, he waited for sight or sound of the **marauders**.

If only on this wild night, in this dark lone spot, he might come across Georg Znaeym, man to man, with no witnesses. That was the wish that was uppermost in his thoughts.

And as he stepped round the trunk of a huge beech, he came face to face with the man he sought.

The two enemies stood glaring at one another for a long, silent moment. Each had a rifle in his hand. Each had hate in his heart and murder uppermost in his mind. The chance had come to let loose the passions of a lifetime.

But a man who has been brought up under the code of a restraining civilization is held in check. He cannot easily nerve himself to shoot down his neighbor in cold blood and without a word except for a crime against his home and honor.

Before their hesitation could give way to action, nature's own violence overwhelmed them both. A fierce shriek of the storm had been answered by a splitting crash over their heads. Before they could leap aside, a huge falling beech tree had thundered down on them.

Ulrich von Gradwitz found himself stretched on the ground. One arm was numb beneath him. The other was held almost as helpless in a tight tangle of forked branches. Both legs were pinned beneath the fallen mass.

His heavy hunting boots had saved his feet from being crushed to pieces. But if his **fractures** were not as serious as they might have been, it was evident that he could not move till someone released him.

The falling twigs had slashed the skin of his face. He had to wink away some drops of blood from his eyelashes before he could get a general view of the disaster.

At his side, so near that under ordinary circumstances he

could almost have touched him, lay Georg Znaeym. Znaeym was alive and struggling but obviously as helplessly **pinioned** as himself. All round them lay a thick wreckage of splintered branches and broken twigs.

Relief at being alive and exasperation at being pinned down in this **plight** brought a strange mix of emotions to Ulrich. Both **pious** thanks and sharp curses rose to his lips.

Georg, who was nearly blinded by blood which trickled across his eyes, stopped his struggling for a moment to listen. Then he gave a short, snarling laugh.

"So you're not killed, as you ought to be. But you're caught, anyway," he cried, "caught fast. Ho, what a jest. Ulrich von Gradwitz snared in his stolen forest. There's real justice for you!"

And he laughed again, mockingly and savagely.

"I'm caught in my own forest land," retorted Ulrich. "When my men come to release us, you may wish that you were in a better situation than being caught poaching. Shame on you!"

Georg was silent for a moment. Then he answered quietly, "Are you sure that your men will find much to release? I have men too in the forest tonight, close behind me. *They* will be here first and do the releasing.

"When they drag me out, it won't need much clumsiness on their part to roll this trunk right over on top of you. Your men will find you dead under a fallen beech tree. For form's sake I shall send my **condolences** to your family."

"It is a useful hint," said Ulrich fiercely. "My men had orders to follow in ten minutes' time. Seven minutes must have gone by already. When they get me out, I will remember the hint. Only since you will have died while poaching on my lands, I don't think I can decently send any condolences to your family."

"Good," snarled Georg, "good. We'll fight this quarrel out to the death—you and I and our foresters. And no cursed

interlopers will come between us. Death and damnation to you, Ulrich von Gradwitz!"

"The same to you, Georg Znaeym, forest thief, game snatcher!"

Both men spoke with the bitterness of possible defeat before them. Each knew that it might be long before his men would seek him out or find him. It was just a matter of chance which party would arrive first on the scene.

Both had now given up the useless struggle to free themselves from the mass of wood that held them down. Ulrich limited his efforts to bringing his one half-free arm near enough to his coat pocket to draw out his wine flask.

Even when he had done this, it was long before he could unscrew the stopper or get any of the liquid down his throat. But what a Heaven-sent sip it seemed!

It was a mild winter, and little snow had fallen as yet. Therefore, the captives suffered less from the cold than might have been the case at that season.

Nevertheless, the wine was warming and **reviving** to the wounded man. He looked across with something like a throb of pity to where his enemy lay. Georg could barely keep the groans of pain and weariness from crossing his lips.

"Could you reach this flask if I threw it over to you?" asked Ulrich suddenly. "There is good wine in it. One may as well be as comfortable as one can. Let us drink, even if tonight one of us dies."

"No, I can scarcely see anything there is so much blood caked round my eyes," said Georg. "In any case I don't drink wine with an enemy."

Ulrich was silent for a few minutes. He lay listening to the weary screeching of the wind.

An idea was slowly forming and growing in his brain. This idea gained strength every time he looked across at the man who was fighting so grimly against pain and exhaustion. In the pain and **languor** that Ulrich himself was feeling, the old fierce hatred seemed to be dying.

"Neighbor," he said presently, "do as you please if your men come first. It was a fair **compact**.

"But as for me, I've changed my mind. If my men are the first to come, you shall be the first to be helped. You will be treated as though you were my guest.

"We have quarreled like devils all our lives over this stupid strip of forest where the trees can't even stand upright in a breath of wind. Lying here tonight, thinking, I've decided that we've been fools really. There are better things in life than winning a quarrel over land.

"Neighbor, if you will help me to bury the old quarrel, I—I will ask you to be my friend."

Georg Znaeym was silent for so long that Ulrich thought he must have fainted from the pain of his injuries. Then he spoke slowly and in jerks.

"How the whole region would stare and chatter if we rode into the market square together. No one living can remember seeing a Znaeym and a Von Gradwitz talking to one another in friendship.

"What peace there would be among the forester folk if we ended our feud tonight," continued Georg. "And if we choose to make peace among our people, there is no one to interfere. No interlopers from outside—

"You would come and keep the Sylvester night[3] beneath my roof. I would come and feast on some holy day at your castle.

"I would never fire a shot on your land, except when you invited me as a guest. And you should come and shoot with me down in the marshes where the wild fowl are.

"In all the countryside, no one could hinder us if we wished to make peace. I never thought I would want to do anything except hate you all my life. But I think I have changed my mind about things too this last half hour. And you offered me your wine flask—

[3]Sylvester night is the eve of December 31. St. Sylvester, bishop of Rome from A.D. 314 to 335, is honored on that night.

"Ulrich von Gradwitz, I will be your friend."

For a space both men were silent. They turned over in their minds the wonderful changes that this dramatic **reconciliation** would bring about. In the cold, gloomy forest, with the wind tearing in fitful gusts through the naked branches and whistling around the trunks, they lay and waited for the help. Now the rescuers would bring release and **succor** to both parties.

And each prayed a private prayer that his men might be the first to arrive. That way he might be the first to show honorable attention to the enemy that had become a friend.

Soon, as the wind dropped for a moment, Ulrich broke the silence.

"Let's shout for help," he said. "In this silence our voices may carry a little way."

"They won't carry far through the trees and undergrowth," said Georg. "But we can try. Together, then."

The two raised their voices in a long hunting call.

"Together again," said Ulrich a few minutes later, after listening in vain for an answering cry.

"I heard something that time, I think," said Ulrich.

"I heard nothing but the damned wind," said Georg hoarsely.

There was silence again for some minutes. Then Ulrich gave a joyful cry.

"I can see figures coming through the wood. They are following the path I took down the hillside."

Both men raised their voices in as loud a shout as they could manage.

"They hear us! They've stopped. Now they see us. They're running down the hill toward us," cried Ulrich.

"How many of them are there?" asked Georg.

"I can't see distinctly," said Ulrich. "Nine or ten."

"Then they are yours," said Georg. "I had only seven

out with me."

"They are making all the speed they can, brave lads," said Ulrich gladly.

"Are they your men?" asked Georg. "Are they your men?" he repeated impatiently as Ulrich did not answer.

"No," said Ulrich with a laugh. It was the idiotic chattering laugh of a man **unstrung** by hideous fear.

"Who are they?" asked Georg quickly. He strained his eyes to see what the other would gladly not have seen.

"*Wolves!*"

"The Interlopers" was first published around 1914.

INSIGHTS INTO SAKI

(1870-1916)

Saki's real name was Hector Hugh Munro (H.H. Munro). He borrowed his pen name from the cupbearer to the gods in Omar Khayyam's poem *The Rubaiyat*.

At 27, Saki followed in his father's footsteps and joined the Burma police. Saki joined the force as a lieutenant because of his father's long career in the police.

But Saki hated being a police officer. Thirteen months, seven fevers, and a case of malaria later, Saki was finally freed from his duty.

Saki had a reputation for being a cruel writer. Indeed, a lot of his stories offer accounts of cruelty.

Since he wrote about such appalling acts, readers often assumed Saki himself was cruel. But this was not the case. His friends knew him as a sensitive man who was actually disgusted by cruelty.

Saki was a great believer in the supernatural. His stories reflect this interest. He sometimes wrote about werewolves, vampires, and ghosts in his tales.

For instance, the title character in Saki's story "Gabriel-Ernest" is human by day and wolf by night. This werewolf admits he preys upon animals and "children when I can get any."

In another Saki story, "The Soul of Leploshka," a miser dies suddenly. He then returns as a ghost to torment a past enemy.

continued

Saki preferred animals to human beings. He respected their acceptance of the law of nature: kill or be killed, eat or be eaten.

When Saki applied this law to humans, he found they could never match the courage shown by animals.

Other works by Saki:

"The Lumber Room," short story
"Mrs. Packletide's Tiger," short story
"The Open Window," short story
"The Schartz-Metterklume Method," short story
"The She-Wolf," short story
"Srendi Vashtar," short story
When William Came, novel
The Death Trap, play

THE MARK OF THE BEAST
RUDYARD KIPLING

VOCABULARY PREVIEW

Below is a list of words that appear in the story. Read the list and get to know the words before you start the story.

annexed—added on or linked up (especially to a larger thing)
certify—to swear to the truth or genuineness of something; guarantee
degradation—downgrading; lowering in class or position
delusion—false belief or opinion
diagnosis—identification by examination
divinity—a god
efficient—effective
endure—bear or tolerate
excessively—extremely; overly
groveling—twisting or crawling face down, usually out of fear or shame
heathen—pagan; not a Jew, Moslem, or Christian
improbable—questionable; unlikely
inference—conclusion reached by reasoning
maniac—mad person
modified—changed, especially to become less powerful or extreme
mystified—puzzled
providence—heavenly protection; God
redress—a payment or deed to make up for a loss
refined—cultured and well-bred
wrathful—angry

THE MARK OF THE BEAST

RUDYARD KIPLING

It is New Year's Eve in colonial India. Time for the proud and rational British soldiers who keep order in the colony to enjoy themselves and party.

Enjoy themselves they do—until one Englishman named Fleete goes too far. During a drunken spree, he offends the Indian natives. But they take revenge with a hair-raising curse: the mark of the beast.

Your gods and my gods—do you or I know which are the stronger?

Native Proverb

Some say that east of the Suez,[1] the direct control of **providence** ceases. There man is handed over to the power of the gods and devils of Asia. The providence of the Church of England is said to exercise only an occasional and **modified** control in the case of Englishmen.

[1]The Suez is the name of a city, gulf, and canal (completed in 1869) in Egypt.

This theory explains some of the more unnecessary honors of life in India. It may be stretched to explain my story.

My friend Strickland of the police knows as much about the natives as is good for any man. He can bear witness to the facts of the case.

Dumoise, our doctor, also saw what Strickland and I saw. The **inference** which he drew from the evidence was entirely incorrect. He is dead now. He died in a rather curious manner. But that has been described elsewhere.

When Fleete came to India, he owned a little money and some land in the Himalayas near a place called Dharmsala. Both properties had been left him by an uncle. Fleete came out to take care of them.

Fleete was a big, heavy, pleasant, and harmless man. His knowledge of natives was limited, of course. He complained, too, about the difficulties of the language.

Fleete rode in from his place in the hills to spend New Year in the station. He stayed with Strickland.

On New Year's Eve there was a big dinner at the club. There was plenty of drinking, naturally. When men gather from the farthest ends of the Empire,[2] they have a right to be wild.

From the frontier came a company of Catch-'em-Alive-O's. These men had not seen twenty white faces a year. They were used to riding fifteen miles at the risk of being shot to reach their dinner and drinks at the next fort.

The troopers profited by their new security. They tried to play pool with a curled-up hedgehog they found in the garden. One of them carried the marker round the room in his teeth.

Half a dozen planters had come in from the south, too. They were talking and boasting to the biggest liar in Asia. He was trying to top all their stories at once.

Everybody was there. And there was a general closing up

---

[2]India was part of the British Empire at the time of the story.

of ranks and taking stock of our losses in dead or injured who had fallen during the past year.

It was a very hard-drinking night. I remember that we sang "Auld Lang Syne" with our feet in the Polo Championship Cup and our heads among the stars. We swore that we were all dear friends.

Then some of us went away and **annexed** Burma. Some tried to open up the Sudan. In turn, they were opened up by Fuzzies in that cruel scrubland.[3]

Some found promotions and medals. Some were married, which was bad. But some did other things which were worse. And the rest of us stayed in our chains and tried to make money on meager experiences.

Fleete began the night with sherry and bitters. He drank champagne steadily up to dessert. Then he switched to raw, rasping Capri with all the strength of whisky.

He went on to take Benedictine with his coffee. To improve his pool game, he downed four or five whiskies and sodas. At half-past two, he drank beer and bones. He wound things up with old brandy.

Consequently, when he came out at half-past three in the morning into fourteen degrees of frost, he was very angry with his horse for coughing. He tried to leapfrog into the saddle. The horse broke away and went to his stables. So Strickland and I formed a guard of dishonor[4] to take Fleete home.

Our road lay through the markets, close to a little temple of Hanuman. Hanuman is a monkey-god and a leading **divinity** worthy of respect.

All gods have good points, just as all priests do. Personally, I regard Hanuman as very important. And I am kind to his people—the great gray apes of the hills. One never

---

[3]Burma, a southeast Asian country, was once a British colony. The Sudan is a northeastern African nation. It was once controlled by the British. In the 1880s, British troops were slaughtered while attempting to put down a revolt in Sudan. "Fuzzies" is an impolite term for blacks who lived in the Sudan.

[4]The narrator is playing on the term "guard of honor." Such a guard is sent to greet or escort an honored person.

knows when one may want a friend.

There was a light in the temple. As we passed, we could hear voices of men chanting hymns. In a native temple the priests rise at all hours of the night to do honor to their god.

Before we could stop him, Fleete dashed up the steps and patted two priests on the back. Then he gravely ground the ashes of his cigar into the forehead of the red stone image of Hanuman.

Strickland tried to drag him out. But Fleete sat down and said solemnly, "Shee that? Mark of the B—beasht! I made it. Ishn't it fine?"

In half a minute the temple was alive and noisy. Strickland, who knew what came of dishonoring gods, said that things might happen. He was known to the priests because of his job, his long residence in the country, and his weakness for associating with the natives. Strickland was feeling unhappy.

Fleete sat on the ground and refused to move. He said that "good old Hanuman" made a very soft pillow.

Then, without any warning, a Silver Man came out of a corner behind the image of the god. He was totally naked in that bitter, bitter cold. His body shone like frosted silver. He was what the Bible calls "a leper as white as snow."[5]

He also had no face. He had been a leper for some years and his disease was far developed.

We two stooped to haul Fleete up. But the temple was filling and filling with folk who seemed to spring from the earth.

Then the Silver Man ran in under our arms. Making a noise exactly like the mewing of an otter, he grabbed Fleete round the body. Before we could wrench him away, the Silver Man had dropped his head on Fleete's. Then he retired to a corner and sat mewing while the crowd blocked all the doors.

[5]A leper is a person with the disease leprosy. Leprosy damages the nerves and can deform the body. It also causes skin to develop lumps and change color. The disease used to be greatly feared. With modern medicine, it now can be treated and stopped in many cases.

The priests were very angry until the Silver Man touched Fleete. That nuzzling seemed to sober them.

At the end of a few minutes' silence one of the priests came to Strickland. In perfect English he said, "Take your friend away. He is done with Hanuman, but Hanuman is not done with him."

The crowd gave room and we carried Fleete into the road.

Strickland was very angry. He said that we might all three have been knifed. He added that Fleete should thank his stars that he had escaped without injury.

Fleete thanked no one. He said that he wanted to go to bed. He was gorgeously drunk.

We moved on. Strickland remained silent and **wrathful**.

Suddenly Fleete was overcome by violent shivering fits and sweating. He said that the smells of the market were overpowering. He wondered what slaughterhouses were permitted so near English homes.

"Can't you smell the blood?" said Fleete.

We put him to bed at last, just as dawn was breaking. Strickland invited me to have another whisky and soda.

While we were drinking he talked of the trouble in the temple. He admitted that it baffled him completely.

Strickland hates being **mystified** by natives. His business in life is to outwit them with their own weapons. He has not yet succeeded in doing this. But in fifteen or twenty years, he will have made some small progress.

"They should have torn us to pieces," he said, "instead of mewing at us. I wonder what they meant. I don't like it one little bit."

I said that the managing committee of the temple would probably have us arrested for insulting their religion. There was a section of the Indian criminal code which exactly fit Fleete's crime. Strickland said he only hoped and prayed that they would do this.

Before I left I looked into Fleete's room. I saw him lying

on his right side, scratching his left breast.

Then I went to bed—cold, depressed, and unhappy—at seven o'clock in the morning.

At one o'clock I rode over to Strickland's house to ask about Fleete's head. I imagined that it would be a sore one.

Fleete was breakfasting and seemed unwell. He had lost his temper. He was yelling at the cook that his chops were not rare enough. A man who can eat raw meat after a night of hard drinking is a curiosity. I told Fleete this and he laughed.

"You breed odd mosquitoes in these parts," he said. "I've been bitten to pieces, but only in one place."

"Let's have a look at the bite," said Strickland. "It may have gone down since this morning."

While the chops were being cooked, Fleete opened his shirt. He showed us a mark just over his left breast. It was the perfect double of the black rosettes—the five or six irregular blotches arranged in a circle—on a leopard's hide.

Strickland looked and said, "It was only pink this morning. It's grown black now."

Fleete ran to a mirror.

"By heaven!" he said, "this is nasty. What is it?"

We could not answer. Just then the chops came in, all red and juicy. Fleete wolfed three down in a most offensive manner. He ate with the right side of his mouth only and threw his head over his right shoulder as he snapped the meat.

When he had finished, it must have struck him that he had behaved strangely. He said apologetically, "I don't think I ever felt so hungry in my life. I've gobbled my meal like an ostrich."

After breakfast Strickland said to me, "Don't go. Stay here, and stay for the night."

Seeing that my house was less than three miles from Strickland's, this request was absurd. But Strickland insisted.

He was about to say something when Fleete interrupted by declaring in a shamefaced way that he felt hungry again.

Strickland sent a servant to my house to fetch over my bedding and a horse. Then we three went down to Strickland's stables to pass the hours until it was time to go out for a ride.

The man who has a weakness for horses never wearies of inspecting them. When two men are killing time in this way, they gather knowledge and lies from one another.

There were five horses in the stables. I shall never forget the scene as we tried to look them over. They seemed to have gone mad. They reared and screamed and nearly tore up their tethers. They sweated and shivered and lathered and were wild with fear.

Strickland's horses used to know him as well as his dogs, which made the matter even stranger.

We left the stable for fear the brutes would hurt themselves in their panic. Then Strickland turned back and called me. The horses were still frightened. But they let us soothe and touch them, and they lay their heads against our chests.

"They aren't afraid of *us,*" said Strickland. "Do you know, I'd give three months' pay if Outrage here could talk."

But Outrage was mute. He could only cuddle up to his master and blow through his nose. That's the custom with horses when they wish to explain things but can't.

Fleete came up when we were in the stalls. As soon as the horses saw him, their fright broke out afresh. It was all that we could do to escape from the place unkicked.

Strickland said, "They don't seem to love you, Fleete."

"Nonsense," said Fleete. "My mare will follow me like a dog."

He went to her; she was in a pen. But as he lifted the bars, she plunged, knocked him down, and broke away into the garden.

I laughed, but Strickland was not amused. He took his moustache in both fists and pulled at it till it nearly came out.

Fleete, instead of going off to chase his property, yawned and said that he felt sleepy. He went to the house to lie down, which was a foolish way of spending New Year's Day.

Strickland sat with me in the stables and asked if I had noticed anything peculiar in Fleete's manner. I said that he ate his food like a beast. But I added that he might have fallen into this habit from living alone in the hills. It was likely when he was out of the reach of society as **refined** and uplifting as ours for instance.

Strickland was not amused. I do not think that he even listened to me. His next sentence referred to the mark on Fleete's breast.

I said that it might have been caused by blister flies. Possibly it was a birthmark newly born and now visible for the first time.

We both agreed that it was unpleasant to look at. And Strickland found the opportunity to say that I was a fool.

"I can't tell you what I think now," said he, "because you would call me a madman. However, you must stay with me for the next few days if you can. I want you to watch Fleete. But don't tell me what you think till I have made up my mind."

"But I am dining out tonight," I said.

"So am I," said Strickland, "and so is Fleete. At least if he doesn't change his mind."

We walked about the garden smoking. We didn't say anything—because we were friends and talking spoils good tobacco—till our pipes were out.

Then we went to wake up Fleete. We found him wide awake and fidgeting about his room.

"I say, I want some more chops," he said. "Can I get them?"

We laughed and said, "Go and change. The ponies will be round in a minute."

"All right," said Fleete. "I'll go when I get the chops—cooked rare, remember."

He seemed to be quite in earnest. It was four o'clock; we had had breakfast at one. Still, for a long time, he demanded those rare chops. Then he changed into riding clothes and went out onto the porch.

His pony—the mare had not been caught—would not let him come near. All three horses were unmanageable—mad with fear. Finally Fleete said that he would stay at home and get something to eat.

Strickland and I rode out wondering. As we passed the temple of Hanuman, the Silver Man came out and mewed at us.

"He is not one of the regular priests of the temple," said Strickland. "I think I should really like to lay my hands on him."

There was no spring in our gallop on the race course that evening. The horses were stale. They moved as though they had been ridden out.

"The fright after breakfast has been too much for them," said Strickland.

That was the only remark he made through the rest of the ride. Once or twice I think he swore to himself, but that did not count.

We came back in the dark at seven o'clock. We saw that there were no lights in the house.

"Careless rascals my servants are!" said Strickland.

My horse reared at something on the drive, and Fleete stood up under its nose.

"What are you doing, **groveling** about the garden?" said Strickland.

But both horses ran and nearly threw us. We dismounted by the stables and returned to Fleete. He was on his hands and knees under the orangebushes.

"What the devil's wrong with you?" said Strickland.

"Nothing, nothing in the world," said Fleete, speaking very quickly and thickly. "I've been gardening—doing some botany, you know. The smell of the earth is delightful. I think I'm going for a walk—a long walk—all night."

Then I saw that there was something **excessively** out of order somewhere. I said to Strickland, "I am not dining out."

"Bless you!" said Strickland. "Here, Fleete, get up. You'll catch a fever there. Come in to dinner and let's have the lamps lit. We'll all dine at home."

Fleete stood up unwillingly and said, "No lamps, no lamps. It's much nicer here. Let's dine outside and have some more chops. Lots of 'em and cooked rare—bloody ones with gristle."

Now a December evening in northern India is bitterly cold. Fleete's suggestion was that of a **maniac**.

"Come in," said Strickland sternly. "Come in at once."

Fleete came. When the lamps were brought, we saw that he was literally plastered with dirt from head to foot. He must have been rolling in the garden.

He shrank from the light and went to his room. His eyes were horrible to look at. There was a green light behind them—not in them, if you understand. And the man's lower lip hung down.

Strickland said, "There is going to be trouble—big trouble—tonight. Don't you change your riding things."

We waited and waited for Fleete's reappearance. In the meantime, we ordered dinner. We could hear him moving about his own room, but there was no light there. Presently from the room came the long-drawn howl of a wolf.

People write and talk lightly of blood running cold and

hair standing up and things of that kind. Both sensations are too horrible to be joked about. My heart stopped as though a knife had been driven through it. Strickland turned as white as the tablecloth.

The howl was repeated. It was answered by another howl far across the fields.

That was the icing on that horrible cake. Strickland dashed into Fleete's room. I followed, and we saw Fleete getting out of the window. He made beast noises in the back of his throat. He could not answer us when we shouted at him. He spat.

I don't quite remember what followed. But I think that Strickland must have stunned him with the long bootjack.[6] Otherwise, I should never have been able to sit on his chest.

Fleete could not speak, he could only snarl. And his snarls were those of a wolf, not of a man.

The human spirit in him must have been giving way all day and have died out with the twilight. We were dealing with a beast that had once been Fleete.

The affair was beyond any human and rational experience. I tried to say "hydrophobia."[7] But the word wouldn't come because I knew that I was lying.

We bound this beast with leather of the punkah[8] rope. Then we tied its thumbs and big toes together and gagged it with a shoehorn. That makes a very **efficient** gag if you know how to arrange it.

Then we carried it into the dining room and sent a man to Dumoise, the doctor, telling him to come over at once.

After we had sent the messenger and were getting our breath, Strickland said, "It's no good. This isn't any work for a doctor."

I knew that he spoke the truth.

The beast's head was free, and it threw it about from side

---

[6]A bootjack is a device shaped like a v and used to pull off boots.

[7]Hydrophobia is another name for rabies.

[8]A punkah is a large Indian fan, often hung from the ceiling and swung back and forth by a rope.

to side. Anyone entering the room would have believed that we were tanning a wolf's skin. That was the most hideous thing of all.

Strickland sat with his chin in his fist. He watched the beast as it wriggled on the ground, but said nothing. The shirt had been torn open in the scuffle. The black rosette mark on the left breast could be seen. It stood out like a blister.

In the silence of the watching we heard something outside mewing like a she-otter. We both rose to our feet. I can't speak for Strickland, but at that sound I felt sick—actually and physically sick. We told each other, as did the men in *Pinafore*,[9] that it was the cat.

Dumoise arrived. I never saw a little man so unprofessionally shocked. He said that it was a heartrending case of hydrophobia and that nothing could be done. Any measures to treat him would only make the agony last longer.

The beast was foaming at the mouth. Fleete, as we told Dumoise, had been bitten by dogs once or twice. Any man who keeps half a dozen terriers must expect a nip now and again.

Dumoise could offer no help. He could only **certify** that Fleete was dying of hydrophobia.

The beast was then howling, for it had managed to spit out the shoehorn. Dumoise said that he would be ready to certify the cause of death and that the end was certain.

He was a good little man, and he offered to remain with us. But Strickland refused the kindness. He did not wish to poison Dumoise's New Year. He would only ask him not to give the real cause of Fleete's death to the public.

So Dumoise left, deeply upset.

As soon as the noise of the cartwheels had died away, Strickland whispered to me his suspicions. They were so

---

[9]*H.M.S. Pinafore* is a comic opera by W.S. Gilbert and Arthur Sullivan. The reference is to a scene where the hero and heroine are trying to escape. When they overhear the noise of pursuers, they try to reassure themselves that it is only a cat.

wildly **improbable** that he dared not say them out loud. And I, who held the same theory, was so ashamed of admitting it that I pretended disbelief.

"Suppose the Silver Man had bewitched Fleete for dishonoring the image of Hanuman? Even so, the punishment could not have fallen so quickly."

As I was whispering this, the cry outside the house rose again. The beast fell into a fresh fit of struggling till we were afraid that the straps that held it would break.

"Watch!" said Strickland. "If this happens six times I shall take the law into my own hands. I order you to help me."

He went into his room. He came out in a few minutes with the barrels of an old shotgun, a fishing line, some thick cord, and his heavy wooden bed frame. I reported that a fit had followed the cry by two seconds in each case. The beast now seemed noticeably weaker.

Strickland muttered, "But he can't take away the life! He can't take away the life!"

I said, though I knew that I was arguing against myself, "It may be a cat. It must be a cat. If the Silver Man is responsible, why does he dare come here?"

Strickland arranged the wood on the hearth and put the gun barrels into the glow of the fire. Then he spread the twine on the table and broke a walking stick in two. There was one yard of fishing line, lapped with wire, and he tied the two ends together in a loop.

Then he said, "How can we catch him? He must be taken alive and unhurt."

I said that we must trust in providence and go out softly with polo sticks into the shrubs at the front of the house. The man or animal that made the cry was evidently moving round the house as regularly as a nightwatchman. We could wait in the bushes till he came by and knock him over.

Strickland accepted this suggestion. We slipped out from

a bathroom window onto the front porch. Then we crossed the drive to the bushes.

In the moonlight we could see the leper coming round the corner of the house. He was totally naked. From time to time he mewed and stopped to dance with his shadow.

It was an unattractive sight. I thought of poor Fleete brought to such **degradation** by so foul a creature. Then I put away all my doubts. I decided to help Strickland. From the heated gun barrels to the loop of twine—from the loins to the head and back again—I would help apply all tortures that might be needed.

The leper halted on the front porch for a moment. Immediately we jumped out on him with the sticks.

He was amazingly strong. We were afraid that he might escape or be fatally injured before we caught him. We had an idea that lepers were frail creatures, but this proved to be incorrect.

Strickland knocked his legs from under him and I put my foot on his neck. He mewed hideously. Even through my riding boots I could feel that his flesh was not the flesh of a clean man.[10]

He struck at us with his hand and feet stumps. We looped the lash of a whip round him, under the armpits. Then we dragged him backwards into the hall and into the dining room where the beast lay. There we tied him with trunk straps. He made no attempt to escape but mewed.

When we confronted him with the beast, the scene was beyond description. The beast doubled backwards into a bow in the most pitiful fashion as though he had been poisoned. Several other things happened also, but they cannot be recorded here.

"I think I was right," said Strickland. "Now we will ask him to cure this case."

But the leper only mewed. Strickland wrapped a towel round his head and took the gun barrels out of the fire. I

---

[10]Strickland and the narrator are careful not to touch the Silver Man. It used to be believed that leprosy could be caught easily by touching a leper.

put the broken walking stick through the loop of fishing line. Then I buckled the leper comfortably to Strickland's bed frame.

I understood then how men and women and little children can **endure** to see a witch burned alive. The beast was moaning on the floor. Though the Silver Man had no face, you could see horrible feelings passing through the slab that took its place. It looked exactly as waves of heat do when they play across red-hot iron—gun barrels for instance.

Strickland shaded his eyes with his hands for a moment and we got to work. This part is not to be printed.

The dawn was beginning to break when the leper spoke. His mewings had not been satisfactory up to that point. The beast had fainted from exhaustion, and the house was very still.

We unstrapped the leper and told him to take away the evil spirit. He crawled to the beast and laid his hand upon the left breast. That was all. Then he fell face down and whincd, drawing in his breath as he did so.

We watched the face of the beast and saw the soul of Fleete coming back into the eyes. A sweat broke out on the forehead and then the eyes—they were human eyes—closed.

We waited for an hour but Fleete still slept. We carried him to his room and ordered the leper to go. To cover his nakedness, we gave him the sheet on the bed. We also gave him the bed frame, the gloves and towels with which we had touched him, and the whip that had been hooked round his body.

He put the sheet about him. Then he went out into the early morning without speaking or mewing.

Strickland wiped his face and sat down. A night gong, far away in the city, rang seven o'clock.

"Exactly twenty-four hours!" said Strickland. "And I've done enough to ensure being dismissed from the service, besides being given a permanent room in a madhouse. Do you believe that we are awake?"

The red-hot gun barrel had fallen on the floor and was singeing the carpet. The smell was entirely real.

That morning at eleven we two together went to wake up Fleete. We looked and saw that the black leopard-rosette on his chest had disappeared.

He was very drowsy and tired. But as soon as he saw us, he said, "Oh! Damn you fellows. Happy New Year to you. Never mix your liquors. I'm nearly dead."

"Thanks for your kindness, but you're a little late," said Strickland. "Today is the morning of the second. You've slept the clock round with a vengeance."

The door opened, and little Dumoise put his head in. He had come on foot. He imagined that we must be tending to Fleete's dead body.

"I've brought a nurse," said Dumoise. "I suppose that she can come in for—what is necessary."

"By all means," said Fleete cheerily, sitting up in bed. "Bring on your nurses."

Dumoise was mute. Strickland led him out and explained that there must have been a mistake in the **diagnosis**. Dumoise remained mute and left the house hastily. He considered that his professional reputation had been injured. He was inclined to take Fleete's recovery as a personal insult.

Strickland went out too. When he came back, he said he had been to the Temple of Hanuman to offer **redress** for the dishonor done to the god. He had been solemnly assured that no white man had ever touched the idol. They also told him he was a man of wonderful virtues, who was suffering from a **delusion**.

"What do you think?" said Strickland.

I said, " 'There are more things—' "[11]

But Strickland hates that quotation. He says that I have worn it threadbare.

One other curious thing happened which frightened me

---

[11]"There are more things in heaven and earth, Horatio, / Than are dreamt of in your philosophy." This is Hamlet's remark to his friend Horatio in Shakespeare's play *Hamlet*.

as much as anything in all the night's work. When Fleete was dressed, he came into the dining room and sniffed. He had a quaint trick of moving his nose when he sniffed.

"Horrid doggy smell, here," said he. "You should really keep those terriers of yours in better order. Try sulfur, Strick."[12]

But Strickland did not answer. He caught hold of the back of a chair. Without warning, he went into an amazing fit of hysterics. It is terrible to see a strong man overtaken with hysteria.

Then it struck me that we had fought for Fleete's soul with the Silver Man in that room and had disgraced ourselves as Englishmen forever. And I laughed and gasped and gurgled just as shamefully as Strickland.

Meanwhile, Fleete thought that we had both gone mad. We never told him what we had done.

Some years later, when Strickland had married and was a churchgoing member of society for his wife's sake, we calmly reviewed the incident. Strickland suggested that I should put it before the public.

I cannot see that this step is likely to clear up the mystery. In the first place, no one will believe a rather unpleasant story.

In the second, it is well known to every right-minded man that the gods of the **heathen** are stone and brass. Any attempt to think of them as anything else is justly condemned.

---

[12]Sulfur can be used to disinfect and deodorize.

"The Mark of the Beast" was first published in 1890.

INSIGHTS INTO
RUDYARD KIPLING

(1865-1936)

Kipling was born in India to English parents. When Kipling was six, he and his younger sister were sent to England to be educated.

The woman young Rudyard lived with abused him. "Aunty Rosa," as she called herself, felt Rudyard was wild and conceited. She was determined to reform him. She often beat him for "showing off." She told him his parents had abandoned him because he was naughty. Once she made him go to school wearing a sign that said "LIAR."

The six years he spent with Aunty Rosa scarred Kipling for life. No one in his family knew how unhappy he had been until he wrote "Baa, Baa, Black Sheep" in 1888. This story was based on his childhood. Ironically, one critic complained that the tale was so brutal it was "not true to life."

Even as a young child, Kipling had very poor eyesight.

Once, on a visit to his aunts and grandmother, Kipling suddenly swung a stick at a tree. When his aunt asked him why, he replied that he "thought it was Grandmama, and had to beat it to see."

His grandmother took him to an eye doctor. From then on, Kipling wore thick glasses.

In those days, it was very unusual for a child to wear glasses. At school, Kipling earned the nickname "Gigger." The other boys called him this because they thought his glasses looked like gig lamps on a horse carriage.

After leaving school, Kipling spent seven years with his parents in India. There he worked as a journalist, writing for a magazine along with his mother, father, and sister. He also wrote several poems and stories, including "The Mark of the Beast."

In 1889, Kipling arrived in London with a bundle of stories to sell. By the end of 1890, he was being described as a "star." What made the difference? In that one year, Kipling had published more than eighty short stories, several poems, and one novel.

In 1889, Kipling traveled through the United States. One of the many stops he made was to visit the famous author Mark Twain.

Twain later recalled that meeting with Kipling. The older, more famous author was surprised by Kipling's brilliant mind and great knowledge.

"He is a most remarkable man—and I am the other one," Twain said. "Between us we cover all knowledge. He knows all that can be known, and I know the rest."

Kipling came to deeply resent reporters and invasions of his privacy.

Once Kipling noticed that a bus often stopped to give tourists a look at his home. Furious, he wrote the bus company to complain. He received no reply, and the buses continued to come.

Kipling wrote another letter, then another. Still the buses arrived regularly.

Finally he stormed into the company's office. "Why do you keep bothering me?" he asked. "Why must I keep on writing you to tell you to stop?"

"That's easy," the company official replied. "I get a lot of money from those letters. I sell them to people who want your signature."

continued

From then on, Kipling was careful about writing unnecessary letters.

Kipling rarely added to his first draft of a story or poem. But he often made the story two or three times shorter through editing.

Kipling liked to refer to this method as "higher editing." After finishing a project, he read it carefully. He would cross out any word that added nothing to his tale.

After Kipling put the story away for a time, he would read and shorten it again. Finally he would read it aloud and make the last cuts.

"I have had tales by me for three or five years," he wrote, "which shortened themselves almost yearly."

Other works by Kipling:
"The Courting of Dinah Shadd," short story
"The Man Who Would Be King," short story
"The Strange Ride of Morrowby Jukes," short story
The Jungle Books, short stories
Just So Stories, short stories
Captains Courageous, novel
Kim, novel

THE ROCKING-HORSE WINNER

D. H. LAWRENCE

VOCABULARY PREVIEW

Below is a list of words that appear in the story. Read the list and get to know the words before you start the story.

arrested—interrupted; halted
brazening—acting boldly and shamelessly
careered—raced or rushed
comparatively—in comparison
divulged—revealed
emancipated—freed; liberated
inspiration—brainstorm; sudden brilliant idea
intruded—interfered; butted in
iridescent—with rainbowlike colors
lucre—money; earnings
materialized—became real; occurred
moderately—somewhat or rather
overwrought—overexcited and very nervous
parried—dodged or sidestepped
remonstrated—protested; objected
smart—stylish and fashionable
stoutly—bravely; courageously
straddled—stood with legs spread wide apart
uncanny—strange and spooky
yarns—stories

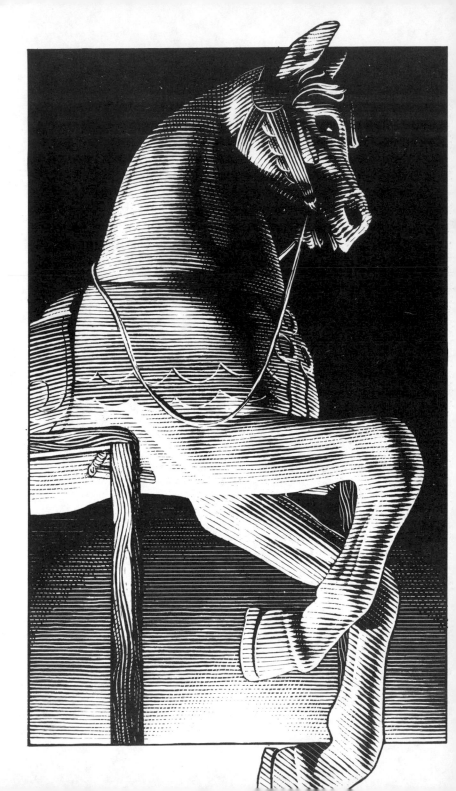

THE ROCKING-HORSE WINNER

Second sight, second chance?

The polished front of Paul's house hides a secret need for money. Paul hears the urgent whispers for cash and finds a way to answer them. It all hinges on a nursery toy . . .

There was a woman who was beautiful. She had started her life with all the advantages, yet she had no luck.

She married for love and the love turned to dust.

She had handsome children. Yet she felt they had been thrust upon her, and she could not love them. They looked at her coldly, as if they were finding

D. H. LAWRENCE

fault with her. And hurriedly she felt she must cover up some fault in herself. Yet she never knew what it was she had to cover up.

Nevertheless, when her children were present, she always felt the center of her heart go hard. This troubled her and made her all the more gentle and anxious for her children. It made it seem she loved them very much.

Only she herself knew that at the center of her heart was a hard little place that could not feel love. No, not for anybody.

Everybody else said, "She is such a good mother. She adores her children." Only she herself, and her children themselves, knew it was not so. They read it in each other's eyes.

There were a boy and two little girls. They lived in a nice house, with a garden, and they had discreet servants. They felt themselves superior to anyone in the neighborhood.

Although they lived in style, they always felt an anxiety in the house. There was never enough money. The mother had a small income, and the father had a small income. But they never had enough to keep up with their social position.

The father went into town to some office. But though he had good chances, these chances never **materialized**. There was always the grinding sense that money was short, though they always kept up their style.

At last the mother said, "I will see if I can't make something." But she did not know where to begin. She racked her brains and tried one thing and another. But she still could not find anything successful.

The failure made deep lines come into her face. Her children were growing up. They would have to go to school. There must be more money, there must be more money.

The father, who had very expensive tastes, seemed as if he would never be able to do anything worth doing. And the mother, who had a great belief in herself, did not succeed any better. Moreover, her tastes were just as expensive.

And so the house came to be haunted by the unspoken phrase: There must be more money! There must be more money!

The children could hear it all the time, though nobody said it aloud. They heard it at Christmas, when the expensive and splendid toys filled the nursery. Behind the shining new rocking horse, behind the **smart** dollhouse, a voice would start whispering. "There must be more money! There must be more money!"

And the children would stop playing to listen for a moment. They would look into each other's eyes to see if they had all heard. And each one saw in the other two that they too had heard.

"There must be more money! There must be more money!"

It came whispering from the springs of the still-swaying rocking horse. Even the horse, bending his wooden head and biting at his harness, heard it. The big doll, sitting so pink and smirking in her new buggy, could hear it plainly. She seemed to be smirking all the more self-consciously because of it.

The foolish puppy, too, looked so very foolish for no other reason than he heard the secret whisper all over the house. "There must be more money!"

Yet nobody ever said it aloud. The whisper was everywhere, and therefore no one spoke it. Just as no one ever says, "We are breathing!" even though we are breathing all the time.

"Mother," said the boy, Paul, one day, "why don't we keep a car of our own? Why do we always use Uncle's or else a taxi?"

"Because we're the poor members of the family," said the mother.

"But why are we, Mother?"

"Well—I suppose," she said slowly and bitterly, "it's because your father has no luck."

The boy was silent for a long time.

"Is luck money, Mother?" he asked, rather timidly.

"No, Paul. Not quite. It's what causes you to have money."

"Oh!" said Paul vaguely. "I thought when Uncle Oscar said filthy lucker, it meant money."

"Filthy **lucre** does mean money," said the mother. "But it's lucre, not luck."

"Oh!" said the boy. "Then what is luck, Mother?"

"It's what causes you to have money. If you're lucky, you have money. That's why it's better to be born lucky than rich. If you're rich, you may lose your money. But if you're lucky, you will always get more money."

"Oh! Will you? And is Father not lucky?"

"Very unlucky, I should say," she said bitterly.

The boy watched her with unsure eyes.

"Why?" he asked.

"I don't know. Nobody ever knows why one person is lucky and another unlucky."

"Don't they? Nobody at all? Does nobody know?"

"Perhaps God. But He never tells."

"He should, then. And aren't you lucky either, Mother?"

"I can't be if I married an unlucky husband."

"But by yourself, aren't you?"

"I used to think I was, before I married. Now I think I am very unlucky indeed."

"Why?"

"Well—never mind! Perhaps I'm not really," she said.

The child looked at her to see if she meant it. But he saw by the line of her mouth that she was only trying to hide something from him.

"Well, anyhow," he said **stoutly**, "I'm a lucky person."

"Why?" said his mother, with a sudden laugh.

He stared at her. He didn't even know why he had said it.

"God told me," he stated, **brazening** it out.

"I hope He did, dear!" she said, again with a laugh but a bitter laugh.

"He did, Mother!"

"Excellent!" said the mother, using one of her husband's exclamations.

The boy saw she did not believe him. Or, rather, that she paid no attention to his claims. This angered him somewhat. It made him want to force her to pay attention.

He went off by himself. Vaguely, in a childish way, he began seeking for the clue to "luck." Wrapped up in this quest, he paid attention to no one. He went about with a sort of secretiveness, seeking inside himself for luck. He wanted luck, he wanted it, he wanted it.

When the two girls were playing dolls in the nursery, he would sit on his big rocking horse, charging madly into space. He would ride with a frenzy that made the little girls peer at him uneasily.

Wildly the horse **careered**. The boy's waving dark hair was tossed. His eyes had a strange glare in them. The little girls dared not speak to him.

When he had ridden to the end of his mad little journey, he climbed down and stood in front of his horse. He stared steadily into its lowered face. Its red mouth was slightly open, its big eye was wide and glassy-bright.

"Now!" he would silently command the snorting steed. "Now, take me to where there is luck! Now take me!"

And he would hit the horse on the neck with a little whip he had asked Uncle Oscar for. He knew the horse could take him where there was luck if only he forced it. So he would mount again and start on his furious ride, hoping to get there at last. He knew he could get there.

"You'll break your horse, Paul!" said the nanny.

"He's always riding like that! I wish he'd stop!" said his

elder sister Joan.

But he only glared down on them in silence. The nanny gave up on him. She could not control him. Anyhow, he was outgrowing her control.

One day his mother and Uncle Oscar came in when he was on one of his furious rides. He did not speak to them.

"Hello, you young jockey! Riding a winner?" said his uncle.

"Aren't you growing too big for a rocking horse? You're not a very little boy any longer, you know," said his mother.

But Paul only gave a blue glare from his big, rather close-set eyes. He would speak to nobody when he was going at full speed. His mother watched him with an anxious expression on her face.

At last he suddenly stopped and slid off.

"Well, I got there!" he announced fiercely. His blue eyes were still flaring and his sturdy long legs were **straddled**.

"Where did you get to?" asked his mother.

"Where I wanted to go," he flared back at her.

"That's right, son!" said Uncle Oscar. "Don't you stop till you get there. What's the horse's name?"

"He doesn't have a name," said the boy.

"Gets along without one all right?" asked the uncle.

"Well, he has different names. He was called Sansovino last week."

"Sansovino, eh? Won the Ascot.[1] How did you know his name?"

"He always talks about horse races with Bassett," said Joan.

The uncle was delighted to find that his small nephew had all the racing news. Bassett was the young gardener, who had been wounded in the left foot during the war. He had gotten this job through Oscar Cresswell after serving as Cresswell's military aid.

---

[1]The Ascot is a horse race. (The Lincoln, Leger, Grand National, and Derby—mentioned later—are also horse races.)

Basset was the perfect example of the "turf"[2] fan. He lived for the races, and the small boy lived with him.

Oscar Cresswell got the whole story from Bassett.

"Master[3] Paul comes and asks me, so I have to tell him, sir," said Bassett. His face was terribly serious, as if he were speaking about religion.

"And does he ever bet anything on a horse he likes?"

"Well—I don't want to betray him. He's a young sport, a fine sport, sir. Would you mind asking him yourself? He sort of takes pleasure in it. And perhaps he'd feel like I was giving him away, sir. If you don't mind."

Bassett was serious as a church.

The uncle went back to his nephew and took him off for a ride in the car.

"Say, Paul, old man, do you ever bet anything on horses?" the uncle asked.

The boy watched the handsome man closely.

"Why; do you think I shouldn't?" he **parried**.

"Not a bit! I thought perhaps you might give me a tip for the Lincoln."

The car sped on into the country. They were on their way to Uncle Oscar's place in Hampshire.

"Word of honor?" said the nephew.

"Word of honor, son!" said the uncle.

"Well, then, Daffodil."

"Daffodil! I doubt it, sonny. What about Mirza?"

"I only know the winner," said the boy. "That's Daffodil."

"Daffodil, eh?"

There was a pause. Daffodil was a long shot, **comparatively**.

"Uncle!"

"Yes, son?"

"You won't let it go any further, will you? I promised Bassett."

[2]The turf is the race track.

[3]Master is a polite term of address for a young boy.

"Bassett be damned, old man! What's he got to do with it?"

"We're partners. We've been partners from the start. Uncle, he loaned me my first five shillings,[4] which I lost. I promised him, word of honor, it was only between me and him.

"But you gave me that ten-shilling note that I started winning with. So I thought you were lucky. You won't let it go any further, will you?"

The boy gazed at his uncle from those big, hot, blue eyes, set close together. The uncle stirred and laughed uneasily.

"Right you are, son! I'll keep your tip private. Daffodil, eh? How much are you betting on him?"

"All except twenty pounds,"[5] said the boy. "I keep that in reserve."

The uncle thought that was a good joke.

"You keep twenty pounds in reserve, do you, you young romancer? What are you betting, then?"

"I'm betting three hundred," said the boy seriously. "But it's between you and me, Uncle Oscar! Word of honor?"

The uncle burst into a roar of laughter.

"It's between you and me all right, you young Nat Gould,"[6] he said, laughing. "But where's your three hundred?"

"Bassett keeps it for me. We're partners."

"You are, are you? And what is Bassett putting on Daffodil?"

"He won't go quite as high as I do, I expect. Perhaps he'll go a hundred and fifty."

"What, pennies?" laughed the uncle.

"Pounds," said the child, with a surprised look at his uncle. "Bassett keeps a bigger reserve than I do."

Between wonder and amusement, Uncle Oscar was silent.

---

[4]Shillings were once British coins.

[5]Pounds are the basic unit of the British currency.

[6]Nat Gould was a British author who wrote numerous novels about horse racing.

He didn't pursue the matter any further. But he decided to take his nephew with him to the Lincoln races.

"Now, son," he said, "I'm putting twenty pounds on Mirza. I'll put five for you on any horse you like. What's your pick?"

"Daffodil, Uncle."

"No, not the five on Daffodil!"

"I would if it was my own five," said the child.

"Good! Good! Right you are! Five for me and five for you on Daffodil."

The child had never been to a race before. His eyes were blue fire. He clenched his mouth tight and watched.

A Frenchman just in front had put his money on Lancelot. Wild with excitement, he waved his arms up and down. He yelled "Lancelot! Lancelot!" in his French accent.

Daffodil came in first, Lancelot second, Mirza third. The child, flushed and eyes blazing, was curiously calm. His uncle brought him four five-pound notes. The odds had been four to one.

"What am I to do with these?" he cried. He waved them in front of the boy's eyes.

"I suppose we'll talk to Bassett," said the boy. "I expect I have fifteen hundred now. And twenty in reserve, plus this twenty."

His uncle studied him for some moments.

"Look here, son!" he said. "You're not serious about Bassett and that fifteen hundred, are you?"

"Yes, I am. But it's between you and me, Uncle. Word of honor!"

"Word of honor all right, son! But I must talk to Bassett."

"If you'd like to be a partner, Uncle, with Bassett and me, we could all be partners. Only you'd have to promise, word of honor, not to let it go beyond us three. Bassett and I are lucky. You must be lucky too. It was your ten shillings

I started winning with—"

Uncle Oscar took both Bassett and Paul into Richmond Park for an afternoon. There they talked.

"It's like this, you see, sir," Bassett said. "Master Paul would get me talking about racing—spinning **yarns**, you know, sir. And he was always intent on knowing if I'd won or lost a bet.

"It's about a year ago, now, that I put five shillings on Blush of Dawn for him—and we lost.

"Then the luck turned with that ten shillings he had from you. We bet that on Singhalese. Since that time, it's been pretty steady, all things considered.

"What do you say, Master Paul?"

"We're all right when we're sure," said Paul. "It's when we're not quite sure that we lose."

"Oh, but we're careful then," said Bassett.

"But when are you sure?" smiled Uncle Oscar.

"It's Master Paul, sir," said Bassett, in a secret, religious voice. "It's as if he had it from heaven. Like Daffodil, now, for the Lincoln. That was as sure as eggs."

"Did you put anything on Daffodil?" asked Oscar Cresswell.

"Yes, sir. I won a bit."

"And my nephew?"

Bassett was stubbornly silent, looking at Paul.

"I made twelve hundred, didn't I, Bassett? I told Uncle I was putting three hundred on Daffodil."

"That's right," said Bassett nodding.

"But where's the money?" asked the uncle.

"I keep it safe. It's locked up, sir. Master Paul can have it any minute he wants to ask for it."

"What, fifteen hundred pounds?"

"And twenty! And forty, that is, with the twenty he made at the race course."

"It's amazing!" said the uncle.

"If Master Paul offers you to be partners, sir, I would if I were you. If you'll excuse me for saying so," said Bassett.

Oscar Cresswell thought about it.

"I'll see the money," he said.

They drove home again. And sure enough, Bassett came round to the garden house with fifteen hundred pounds in bills. The twenty pounds reserve was left with Joe Glee at the Turf Commission.

"You see, it's all right, Uncle, when I'm sure! Then we go strong, for all we're worth. Don't we, Bassett?"

"We do that, Master Paul."

"And when are you sure?" said the uncle, laughing.

"Oh, well, sometimes I'm absolutely sure—like about Daffodil," said the boy. "And sometimes I have an idea. And sometimes I haven't even an idea, have I, Bassett? Then we're careful, because we mostly lose."

"You do, do you! And when you're sure—like about Daffodil—what makes you sure, sonny?"

"Oh, well, I don't know," said the boy uneasily. "I'm just sure, Uncle; that's all."

"It's as if he had it from heaven, sir," Bassett repeated.

"I should say so!" said the uncle.

But he became a partner. And when the Leger was coming up, Paul was "sure" about Lively Spark. Lively Spark was quite a long shot. But the boy insisted on putting a thousand on the horse. Bassett went for five hundred, and Oscar Cresswell went two hundred.

Lively Spark came in first. The odds had been ten to one against him. Paul had made ten thousand.

"You see," he said, "I was absolutely sure of him."

Even Oscar Cresswell had made two thousand.

"Look here, son," he said, "this makes me nervous."

"It doesn't need to, Uncle! Perhaps I won't be sure again for a long time."

"But what are you going to do with your money?" asked

the uncle.

"Of course, I started it for Mother," said the boy. "She said she had no luck because Father is unlucky. So I thought if I was lucky, it might stop whispering."

"What might stop whispering?"

"Our house. I hate our house for whispering."

"What does it whisper?"

"Why—why," the boy fidgeted, "why, I don't know. But it's always short of money, you know, Uncle."

"I know it, son, I know it."

"You know people send Mother writs,[7] don't you, Uncle?"

"I'm afraid I do," said the uncle.

"And then the house whispers, like people laughing at you behind your back. It's awful, it is! I thought if I was lucky—"

"You might stop it," added the uncle.

The boy watched him with big blue eyes that had an **uncanny** cold fire in them. He said not a word.

"Well, then!" said the uncle. "What are we doing?"

"I wouldn't like Mother to know I was lucky," said the boy.

"Why not, son?"

"She'd stop me."

"I don't think she would."

"Oh!" The boy squirmed in an odd way. "I don't want her to know, Uncle."

"All right, son! We'll manage it without her knowing."

They managed it very easily. At his uncle's suggestion, Paul handed over the thousand pounds. His uncle deposited it with the family lawyer.

The lawyer was to inform Paul's mother that a relative had put five thousand pounds into his hands. That sum was to be paid out, a thousand pounds at a time, on the mother's birthday for the next five years.

[7]A writ is a written order issued by a court. It orders a person to do something or stop doing something. Here the writ is probably a warning to pay a debt.

"So she'll have a birthday present of a thousand pounds for five years in a row," said Uncle Oscar. "I hope it won't make it all the harder for her later."

Paul's mother had her birthday in November. The house had been "whispering" worse than ever lately. Even in spite of his luck, Paul could not bear up against it. He was very anxious to see his mother's reaction to the birthday letter, telling her about the thousand pounds.

When there were no visitors, Paul now took his meals with his parents. He had outgrown the nursery.

His mother went into town nearly every day. She had discovered that she had an odd knack for sketching furs and dresses. She worked secretly in a friend's studio who was the chief "artist" for the leading clothing stores. She drew the figures of ladies in furs and silk and sequins for the newspaper ads.

This young woman artist earned several thousand pounds a year. But Paul's mother only made several hundreds. Again she was dissatisfied. She so wanted to be first in something. And she did not succeed even in making sketches for clothing ads.

She came down to breakfast on the morning of her birthday. Paul watched her face as she read her letters. He knew which one was the lawyer's letter.

As his mother read it, her face hardened and became more expressionless. Then a cold determined look came on her mouth. She hid the letter under the pile of others and didn't say a word about it.

"Didn't you have anything nice in the mail for your birthday, Mother?" said Paul.

"Quite **moderately** nice," she said. Her voice was cold and distant.

She went away to town without saying more.

But in the afternoon Uncle Oscar appeared. He said Paul's mother had had a long interview with the lawyer. She asked if the whole five thousand could be given to her at once because she was in debt.

"What do you think, Uncle?" said the boy.

"I leave it to you, son."

"Oh, let her have it, then! We can get some more with the other," said the boy.

"A bird in the hand is worth two in the bush, lad!" said Uncle Oscar.

"But I'm sure to know about the Grand National. Or the Lincolnshire. Or else the Derby. I'm sure to know for one of them," said Paul.

So Uncle Oscar signed the agreement, and Paul's mother got the whole five thousand.

Then something very curious happened. The voices in the house suddenly went mad, like a chorus of frogs on a spring evening.

There were certain new pieces of furniture, and Paul had a tutor. He was really going to Eton,[8] his father's school, in the following autumn. There were flowers in the winter. The luxury that Paul's mother had been used to blossomed again.

Yet the voices in the house, behind the beautiful flowers and from under the **iridescent** cushions, screamed in delight. "There must be more money! Oh-h-h, there must be more money. Oh, now now-w! Now-w-w—there must be more money! More than ever! More than ever!"

It frightened Paul terribly. He studied away at his Latin and Greek with his tutor. But his intense hours were spent with Bassett. The Grand National had gone by. He had not "known" and had lost a hundred pounds.

Summer was at hand. He was in agony for the Lincoln. But even for the Lincoln he didn't "know," and he lost fifty pounds.

He became wild-eyed and strange. It seemed as if something were going to explode in him.

---

[8]Eton is a famous school in England that prepares students for college. Many rich families send their sons to Eton.

"Let it alone, son! Don't you bother about it!" urged Uncle Oscar. But it was as if the boy couldn't hear what his uncle was saying.

"I've got to know for the Derby! I've got to know for the Derby!" the child repeated. His big blue eyes were blazing with a sort of madness.

His mother noticed how **overwrought** he was.

"You'd better go to the seaside. Wouldn't you like to go now to the seaside instead of waiting? I think you'd better," she said, anxiously. Her heart was curiously heavy because of him.

But the child lifted his uncanny blue eyes.

"I couldn't possibly go before the Derby, Mother!" he said. "I couldn't possibly!"

"Why not?" she said. Her voice was heavy as always when someone argued with her.

"Why not? You can still go from the seaside to the Derby with Uncle Oscar if you wish. No need for you to wait here.

"Besides, I think you care too much about these races. It's a bad sign. My family has been a gambling family. You won't know till you grow up how much damage it's done. But it has done damage.

"I will have to send Bassett away and ask Uncle Oscar not to talk racing to you unless you promise to be reasonable about it.

"Go away to the seaside and forget it. You're all nerves!"

"I'll do what you like, Mother. Just don't send me away till after the Derby," the boy said.

"Send you away from where? Just from this house?"

"Yes," he said, gazing at her.

"Why, you curious child! What makes you care about this house so much, suddenly? I never knew you loved it."

He looked at her without speaking. He had a secret within a secret. It was something he had not **divulged** even to Bassett or Uncle Oscar.

His mother stood undecided and a little bit sad for some moments.

Then she said, "Very well! Don't go to the seaside till after the Derby if you don't wish.

"But promise me you won't let your nerves go to pieces. Promise you won't think so much about horse racing and 'events,' as you call them!"

"Oh, no," said the boy casually. "I won't think much about them, Mother. You needn't worry. I wouldn't worry, Mother, if I were you."

"If you were me and I were you," said his mother, "I wonder what we should do!"

"But you know you needn't worry, Mother, don't you?" the boy repeated.

"I would be awfully glad to know it," she said wearily.

"Oh, well, you can, you know. I mean, you should know you don't need to worry," he insisted.

"Should I? Then I'll see about it," she said.

Paul's secret of secrets was his wooden horse that had no name. Since being **emancipated** from his nannies, he had had his rocking horse moved to his bedroom at the top of the house.

"Surely, you're too big for a rocking horse!" his mother had **remonstrated**.

"Well, Mother, till I can have a real horse, I like to have some sort of animal around," had been his quaint answer.

"Do you feel he keeps you company?" she laughed.

"Oh, yes! He's very good. He always keeps me company when I'm there," said Paul.

So the horse, rather shabby, stood in an **arrested** prance in the boy's bedroom.

The Derby was drawing near. The boy grew more and more tense. He hardly heard what was spoken to him. He was very frail, and his eyes were really uncanny.

His mother had sudden seizures of worry about him.

Sometimes, for half an hour, she would feel a sudden anxiety about him that was almost despair. She wanted to rush to him at once and know he was safe.

Two nights before the Derby, she was at a big party in town. Suddenly one of those rushes of anxiety about her boy, her firstborn, overcame her. It gripped her heart till she could hardly speak. She fought with the feeling with all her might, for she believed in common sense. But the feeling was too strong. She had to leave the dance and go downstairs to telephone to the country.

The children's governess[9] was terribly surprised at being called in the night.

"Are the children all right, Miss Wilmot?"

"Oh yes, they are quite all right."

"Master Paul? Is he all right?"

"He was right as rain when he went to bed. Shall I run up and look at him?"

"No," said Paul's mother reluctantly. "No! Don't trouble. It's all right. Don't sit up. We shall be home fairly soon." She did not want her son's privacy **intruded** upon.

"Very good," said the governess.

It was about one o'clock when Paul's mother and father drove up to their house. All was still. Paul's mother went to her room and slipped off her white fur coat. She had told her maid not to wait up for her. She heard her husband downstairs, mixing a whisky and soda.

And then, because of the strange anxiety in her heart, she stole upstairs to her son's room. Silently she went along the upper hallway. Was there a faint noise? What was it?

With arrested muscles, she stood, outside his door, listening. There was a strange, heavy, and yet not loud noise. Her heart stood still. It was a soundless noise, yet rushing and powerful. Something huge was in violent, hushed motion. What was it? What in God's name was it? She should

---

[9]A governess is a woman paid to teach the children of one family.

know. She felt that she knew the noise. She knew what it was.

Yet she could not place it. She couldn't say what it was. And on and on it went, like a madness.

Softly, frozen with anxiety and fear, she turned the doorknob.

The room was dark. Yet in the area near the window, she heard and saw something plunging to and fro. She gazed in fear and amazement.

Then, suddenly, she switched on the light. She saw her son, in his green pajamas, madly riding the rocking horse. The blaze of light suddenly lit him up as he urged the wooden horse.

It lit her up, too, as she stood in the doorway, blonde and in her dress of pale green and crystal.

"Paul!" she cried. "Whatever are you doing?"

"It's Malabar!" he screamed, in a powerful, strange voice. "It's Malabar."

His eyes blazed at her for one strange and senseless second as he ceased urging his wooden horse. Then he fell with a crash to the ground.

All the tormented feelings of motherhood flooded over her. She rushed to take him in her arms.

But he was unconscious. And unconscious he remained with some brain fever. He talked and tossed, and his mother sat stonily by his side.

"Malabar! It's Malabar! Bassett, Bassett, I know! It's Malabar!"

So the child cried, trying to get up and urge the rocking horse that gave him his **inspiration**.

"What does he mean by Malabar?" asked the heart-frozen mother.

"I don't know," said the father stonily.

"What does he mean by Malabar?" she asked her brother Oscar.

"It's one of the horses running for the Derby," was the answer.

And, in spite of himself, Oscar Cresswell spoke to Bassett. He himself put a thousand on Malabar. The odds were fourteen to one.

The third day of the illness was critical. They were waiting for a change. The boy, with his long, curly hair, was tossing endlessly on the pillow. He neither slept nor regained consciousness. And his eyes were like blue stones. His mother sat, feeling her heart had gone. It was as though it had actually turned to stone.

In the evening Oscar Cresswell did not come. But Bassett sent a message. He wanted to come up for a moment, if he could.

Paul's mother was very angry at the intrusion. On second thought, she agreed. The boy was the same. Perhaps Bassett might bring him to consciousness.

The gardener was a short fellow with a little brown mustache and sharp little brown eyes. He tiptoed into the room and touched his imaginary cap to Paul's mother.

Then he crept to the bedside. He stared with glittering, small eyes at the tossing, dying child.

"Master Paul!" he whispered. "Master Paul! Malabar came in first all right, a clean win.

"I did as you told me. You've made over seventy thousand pounds, you have. You've got over eighty thousand. Malabar came in all right, Master Paul."

"Malabar! Malabar! Didn't I tell you Malabar, Mother? Didn't I tell you Malabar? Do you think I'm lucky, Mother? I knew Malabar, didn't I?

"Over eighty thousand pounds! I call that lucky, don't you, Mother? Over eighty thousand pounds! I knew, didn't I know I knew? Malabar came in all right.

"I just must ride my horse till I'm sure. Then I tell you, Bassett, you can bet as much as you like. Did you bet all your money, Bassett?''

"I went a thousand on it, Master Paul."

"I never told you, Mother. If I can ride my horse and get there, then I'm absolutely sure—oh absolutely! Mother, did I ever tell you? I am lucky."

"No, you never did," said the mother.

But the boy died in the night.

And even as he lay dead, his mother heard her brother's voice.

"My God, Hester, you're eighty thousand pounds to the better. And a poor devil of a son to the worse. But, poor devil, poor devil, it's best he's out of a life where he rides his rocking horse to find a winner."

"The Rocking-Horse Winner" was first published in 1933.

INSIGHTS INTO
D. H. LAWRENCE

(1885-1930)

Those initials? They stand for David Herbert.

Lawrence's childhood friend, Jessie Chambers, caused Lawrence's first literary success. Without telling the author, Jessie copied Lawrence's poems. Then he secretly sent the work to the *English Review*. This was the best literary magazine of the time.

Editor Ford Madox Ford instantly recognized Lawrence's talent.

"I've discovered a genius," he announced at a dinner of famous writers. "He is called D.H. Lawrence."

Soon the whole literary circle was speaking about Lawrence. They were anxious to read his work. The November 1909 edition of the *English Review* gave them that chance. That issue alone contained six poems by Lawrence.

Lawrence was a skillful impersonator. He would stage one-man shows for his wife, Frieda, when she was feeling low. Sometimes he also entertained guests with his talent.

Lawrence imitated such famous writers as Ezra Pound and W.B. Yeats. He also poked fun at himself. "Lawrence charming his landlady. Lawrence being put in his place by his landlady's daughter. A bad-tempered Lawrence picking a fight with Frieda over nothing," were the names of some of the scenes he enacted.

These skits usually had his audience rolling on the floor in helpless laughter.

continued

The entire first edition of Lawrence's novel, *The Rainbow,* was destroyed by court order. The book was judged to be indecent and obscene. But that may not have been the only reason the novel was banned.

Lawrence published *The Rainbow* in 1915. That year the English were fighting for their lives in World War I. And Lawrence's novel featured characters who criticized England. They talked unpatriotically of war and rebelled against England's society.

These attitudes probably played a part in the decision to destroy all copies of *The Rainbow.*

As a child, Lawrence saw the endless clash between his working-class father and uppercrust mother. Lawrence always sided with his mother and grew to hate his father.

His father worked in the coal mines. After work, he usually headed for the bar. This left his wife responsible for picking up his paycheck.

But Mrs. Lawrence refused to stand in that working-class line. The task was left to her sons.

When Lawrence was old enough, he inherited the duty. But he dreaded going. He hated the cashier, who would always tease him.

"Where's your pa, lad?" he would ask Lawrence. "Too drunk to collect the pay himself?"

This cruel taunt only strengthened Lawrence's hate for his father and devotion toward his mother.

Lawrence once saved a woman friend from a total mental breakdown. The woman's affair with a man ended in tragedy when the man committed suicide. After his death, her own will to live was gone.

Lawrence was determined to heal his friend. However, he did not try to make her forget her sorrow. Instead, he fed it by reading Greek tragedies with her. He hoped she would recover by accepting that life brings pain and grief to every human.

The woman's tragedy also had its effect on Lawrence. The incident inspired him to write *The Trespasser*.

Lawrence was angered by the American publication of *Sons and Lovers*. He received nothing from its publication—not a single dollar.

Ten years later, Lawrence was still complaining. He always said that America had read his most popular book for free.

Other works by Lawrence:
"The Fox," short story
"The Horse Dealer's Daughter," short story
"Odor of Chrysanthemums," short story
"St. Mawr," short story
"Snake," poem
"Tortoise Shout," poem
Lady Chatterley's Lover, novel
Sons and Lovers, novel
Women in Love, novel